# Stiff Competition: A Winter Cozy Special

## Iris Leigh

Cover Design: KDS Cover Concepts

# Stiff Competition: A Winter Cozy Special

**A ski resort. A dead ex. A race to prove my innocence.**

After the humiliation my ex-boyfriend put me through, I need a break. A ski vacation high in the mountains is in order, and I couldn't be more thrilled. Two hours from civilization and a hundred miles away from my troubles.

But my hopes for a fun and relaxing vacation come to a screeching halt on the second day when my ex-boyfriend is found dead. Now everyone thinks I'm to blame.

Instead of enjoying time on the slopes, I'll spend every waking moment fighting to clear my name and find the person responsible for his murder.

That would be a lot easier if relationships weren't so fickle and the who's who of assorted lovers, spurned wives, and a soon-to-be police officer wasn't making my life so complicated.

**Can I clear my name before it's too late?**

To Winter,

My favorite season, you are dearly missed. I shall be leaving the south soon, it's too hot down here.

# Contents

# Chapter One

I rubbed my hands together as I brought them closer to my face in order to blow on them. I had to remove my gloves several times outside while on the slopes. It felt like the cold was piercing my skin. A shiver coursed through me as we waited in line for refreshments. My body was warming up, but a girl from Florida who took a trip to a winter resort ... probably not the best combination.

But you only live once, so why not?

"I can't wait to get some hot apple cider and curl up next to the fireplace," Sophia said next to me. I turned to face her as her long, wavy brown hair swayed from side to side as she kept wiggling to warm her body up. We were both feeling the impact of being outside for too long, and a few cups of hot apple cider would certainly do the trick.

"Tell me again why I agreed to go on this trip with you? I'm absolutely freezing my butt off up here!" she hollered, shooting me a glare. Her little hops from side to side never stopped and all I could do was laugh. It was a last-minute trip up to the mountains to escape all the horrible things that kept happening back home. Finding my boyfriend cheating on me with another girl ... that was the final straw ... and that was exactly how I found myself freezing my butt off up in the mountain with my best friend.

"It's not that bad up here. Maybe I should move up here?"

Sophia's head whipped in my direction to stare at me. She was a whole head taller than me, so I craned up to meet her stare. It was silent as we both shifted forward a few steps in line as the employees behind the counter finished assisting another person.

"Good one, Britt, I almost thought you were for real," she laughed, her arms coming to wrap around her stomach.

"I wasn't joking," I mumbled, annoyed that she didn't think I had what it took to survive up here.

"Trust me, you were. You up here longer than a week? Don't be crazy."

"I'm not being crazy!" I huffed as I crossed my arms. "Shouldn't you be supporting me instead of laughing?" I shot back, but it had no bite, for a smile was present on my face.

"What do you call hauling my butt up here to the cold, then? If I didn't know any better, I would say that makes me a great friend."

I latched on to Sophia's arm as we finally made it to the counter to order some drinks. The laughing had helped, but the hot apple cider would certainly be the last drop in the bucket to send warmth soaring through my body.

"What can I get for you ladies?" the man asked from behind the counter.

"Two large apple ciders please," I answered.

"Add two slices of pizza and a large order of fries as well," Sophia said. I rolled my eyes at her. We would be going to dinner later on, but after being outside and being cold, I guess she had worked up an appetite. Hopefully, she would share her food.

The total flashed on the register. I grimaced at the price. If there was one thing about taking a vacation to a ski resort, it wasn't cheap; they charged an arm and a leg for the food. After all, where else would we get it from? The only way down the mountain was with the shuttle service, and it only ran during certain hours. Plus, being on a bus for several hours was not how I wanted to spend my relaxation time.

I forked over my credit card, which the attendant promptly returned. There was a part of me inside that had hoped it would have declined so I wouldn't have to pay. It wasn't the case, though.

"Keeping you fed is causing a huge dent in my pocket."

"But you wouldn't have it any other way," Sophia responded, and I let out a sigh. It's true, I wouldn't have it any other way. I needed the girls' trip with her to get my mind off of being cheated on. I maneuvered over to the end of the counter, where our food was being piled onto a tray for easy mobility. With a quick scan of the small lodge food court, I spied an empty table only a few paces away from a fireplace already lit and crowded by other lodge residents. I sighed; we wouldn't be sitting outside on the deck tonight. Even though there were bonfires on the deck, nothing would beat the combination of a fireplace and actual heating.

"Here you go. Enjoy," the man working said, his voice muffled as he kept working. With a quick thank you shot in his direction, I grabbed our tray and headed over to the table to claim it before someone else did.

"Will you tell me the story once more? Of how you caught Matt?" Sophia asked as she reached out and plucked a few French fries from the tray.

"Why do you like hearing this story?"

"It's funny."

"I'm glad my misery makes you laugh."

Sophia shot me a smile before grabbing a few more fries from the plate as we finally made our way to the table.

"Well, it was like any other hot humid night in Florida."

"Oh, we doing storyteller mode?" she said as she picked up a pizza slice with one hand and held her apple cider with the other.

"Do you want to hear the story or not?"

She motioned with her pizza for me to continue. I rolled my eyes at her antics. Sophia was a different breed.

"Like I said, it was just a normal hot, humid night. I was watching a movie, something scary I think, when my phone rang. It was Matt's mother asking if I could over to help with something."

"That should have been alarm bell number one," Sophia chimed in, interrupting my story, taking a bite of her pizza. "Why is she calling you and not her son? You guys only met a few times."

"I think nothing of it. Who wouldn't want their boyfriend's mom to like them? So I head over and she has me doing some mundane tasks around the house. Again, I think nothing of it as I help her out."

"I'm not sure I should be impressed by your stupidity or be concerned," Sophia said as she finally finished off the first pizza and dived into the fries on the table.

"Yeah, yeah. Love makes people blind. Anyway, I'm helping his mother when she takes a phone call and goes to another room, but I still can hear. She is talking to Matt about the proposal he is setting up for, how's it going, and that she is running out of things for me to do."

"Here I was, thinking my boyfriend was going to propose! So I was trying to act cool and pretend I didn't hear anything, you know?" I slumped back in my chair.

The worst part of the story was finally about to arrive.

"We finally finished, and she asks for one more task, but in order to do it we had to drive somewhere, so I'm like, of course! We pile into her car and arrive at the beach. At this point I'm beyond excited and a little sad that I couldn't get dressed up, but it was a surprise after all."

"Here is the best part!" Sophia exclaimed as she continued to down the fries on the table. I rolled my eyes, but she was right. The best part was about to come.

"We arrive at the beach and Matt is there. He walks up to us and gets down on one knee. He pauses and looks at his mother—and let me say when he spoke I thought I died inside. He asked his mother why I was there and his mother was like what do you mean?" I exclaimed, as I did my best to reproduce their own voices to help the story along.

"Then Matt has the audacity to say to his mother that she brought the wrong girlfriend. WRONG GIRLFRIEND?" My voice was getting louder, but I didn't care. It still irked me thinking about what had unfolded. "The mother looks to me and then asks who I am! Like what in the world is going on? But I was in a daze and I answered her ridiculous question with my name."

"Exactly why I was wondering if I should be impressed or concerned."

"Stop interrupting the story! Where was I? Right, I said I was Brittany because that is who I am. But his mother was still looking at me like she didn't know a Brittany. Like I just didn't spend the last two hours helping around the house. Now I'm super confused on what is going on, and Matt ushers me away from his puzzled mother back up the beach and to the sidewalk. The whole time he is apologizing about his mother and that this is just a big misunderstanding. He waves over a taxi and ushers me in the car, tells me he will call me later, then sends me on my way..." I let out a big sigh. "It wasn't the brightest moment of my life, but I was a girl in shock."

Sophia took a sip of her apple cider as her head shook from side to side to show her disappointment. Before she snorted and some of the liquid sprayed out, her snort morphed into a full blow laugh.

"All you managed to say was I'm Brittany, and they sent you on your merry way without another peep out of you."

"I know ... I know. It was horrible."

"And he called you the next day, right?"

"Yeah, and texted asking if I wanted breakfast. I know I wasn't crazy and the night before was still vivid in my mind, so I blocked him."

"I don't know about the not crazy part, but good for you."

I grabbed the last slice of pizza that Sophia had thankfully not touched during the story. All the fries were gone, but that was okay, we would be eating dinner later on anyways. This was just a snack to hold us over. With my lukewarm apple cider in one hand and the pizza in the other, I finally sat back to wind down from the day. What had happened between Matt and me was an unfortunate situation and should be kept to the movies and out of real life.

"AHH!!!" A scream pierced through the air, pausing me from taking a big chuck out of the pizza. My stomach grumbled at the displeasure of putting the pizza back on the plate, but someone needed help. I looked around, trying to find the source of the scream. I wasn't the only person looking; others started to scramble. Everyone seemed to be drifting towards the outside deck area, so that seemed to be where something was going on.

"Let's go," I said to Sophia, who looked at me for a minute.

"I'm pretty sure you are supposed to run away from trouble, not to it."

I paid her no mind as I grabbed her hand and yanked her from the chair, pulling her towards the source of the scream. I wasn't sure what was going on, but we would soon find out.

# Chapter Two

There was a crowd on the deck. It was a great place for people to cozy up next to the fire pits and enjoy the view of the mountain. Except this time, no one was enjoying the view, for something in the center of the circle held everyone's full attention, and I wanted to see what it was. What had caused some lady to scream as if she were being murdered? Whatever was unfolding seemed like the perfect chance to bury any thoughts about Matt.

"Excuse me, do you know what is going on?" I asked the nearest person, who quickly shook their head, looking back into the crowd. I pursed my lips. The woman was still wailing. I couldn't see over the crowd. But I needed to get closer in order to satisfy my curiosity. Without hesitation, I maneuvered Sophia in front of me and pushed her forward, latching on to her to make sure we wouldn't get separated as we pushed our way through. Her heels dug into the flooring in an attempt to stop me, but I just kept pushing. She might be taller than me, but she wasn't stronger.

"What are you doing?" she hissed as she accepted defeat and started to walk on her own.

"Trying to get closer. What do you think?" I answered as I jumped on my tippy toes to look over her shoulder.

"You couldn't leave me out of it?"

"We are on this trip together, so shouldn't we go together to see what is going on?"

"What kind of logic is that? That shouldn't apply when someone is screaming bloody murder!" she bit back.

Once my interest was satisfied, we could go back to eating and doing whatever Sophia wanted.

Pain surged in my nose as I slammed right into the back of my best friend. One moment she was walking with very little persuasion from me, then suddenly she was a solid rock.

"What's going on?" I asked as I jabbed her forward, but this time she pushed back. She whirled on me and cuffed her hands on my elbows, shifting me around to face away from the center of the crowd. This time it was Sophia pushing me, but all that did was pique my curiosity more. What had spooked Sophia and sent her running with her tail between her legs?

With a quick lunge to the left, I swirled on my feet and darted to the right, a smile on my face. Sophia had already seen what was in the center. All I needed was a quick peek and I would be content.

"Don't," Sophia called out as she tried to grab on to me. All that did though was push me tumbling through the crowd as I backed away from her grasp. What was up with her?

My knees slammed into the ground as I fell the rest of the way through the crowd straight to the center. I dragged my eyes up from the wooden deck to see the body of a man. My own body froze just like the body before me. Had someone died? How? Thoughts of just having a quick peek were smothered by the dozen questions as I tried to understand the situation.

My eyes darted to the woman who was holding the man's head. Her light blue eyes twinkled with tears as they ran down her cheeks. It was starting to smear the eyeliner around her eyes. I scrunched my nose. She should probably invest in waterproof eyeliner, but I bet she hadn't expected to be crying during her trip. Poor girl. But who was the person dead on the ground?

My eyes drifted down and my blood ran cold, for a very familiar face was present. It was Matt, but what was he doing here? Most importantly: why was he dead?

Someone broke through the crowd and threw out a sheet to cover my ex-boyfriend from view, but the damage was done. Matt was dead. Hands grasped my elbow and pulled me away from the center of the crowd. Wide eyed, I looked at Sophia. Now I knew exactly why she was spooked and didn't want me to continue forward.

"What is Matt doing here?" I hissed to her as I tried to wrap my mind around what was going on. If only I wasn't a curious being, I would have been saved the trouble of seeing him.

"I don't know, he is your ex-boyfriend, not mine," she whispered, but it wasn't silent enough, for the man we were about to push past stopped us. He was taller than both myself and Sophia as I craned my head up to look at him.

"That man is your ex-boyfriend?" he asked, his deep voice overpowering the other noises from the crowd, but his question quickly silenced all chatter. I could feel eyes on me as people shifted beside us to stare at Sophia and us.

"What does it matter to you?" Sophia said as she attempted to make herself look big. She couldn't fight to save her life, but people didn't know that.

"We got a dead guy and an ex-girlfriend. If you put the pieces together, it is looking awfully suspicious," he said, arms crossed over his chest, peering down at us.

"Who are you?" a female voice chimed in from behind, and I turned. With her long black hair, blue eyes and smeared makeup, it wasn't hard to identify who it was; I had just seen her moments ago cradling the body of Matt. I didn't know her name, but she was probably his new girlfriend, and maybe even the one who he was supposed to propose to that night on the beach.

"I'm Brittany. I'm his ex-girlfriend, but we broke up a few days ago."

"That's impossible."

"Look, I'm not trying to cause any trouble. I was just curious to see what was going on. I didn't even know he was here."

I brought my hands up and waved them to help dismiss the tension. I really didn't know he was here, I traveled up this mountain to get away from him after all.

"You're lying," she bit back.

"Who are you to say she is lying?" Sophia exclaimed as I felt her move from behind me.

"I'm Olivia, his wife!" she hollered as she brought up her hand to show the very large rock on her finger. I looked from the diamond to her smeared makeup and back to the diamond. Matt had a wife? Did they elope or something? That was a very fast engagement period.

"I thought you said he had a fiancée," Sophia attempted to whisper, but the shock in her voice didn't help muffle her question.

"That's what I thought. Maybe they got married fast?"

"What are you talking about? We have been married for five years," the lady said. The gears that were once working overtime to try to piece things together slammed to a halt. Information kept flowing out into the world but I could no longer process it. Matt and I had broken up because he was cheating on me and planned to marry another woman. But he was already married? And we somehow all of us ended up on the same mountain where Matt just happened to drop dead? Yeah, nothing was making sense.

"If you're his wife, who was he proposing to?" Sophia asked, but I couldn't answer her question, for I had no clue as well.

"What happened to my fiancé?" a new voice pierced the air as I peered around Matt's wife. There on the ground was a woman with fiery red hair who had lifted up the blanket to peer at the face of the body underneath. It seemed Matt had a thing for over-curious types. She dropped the blanket and whirled on us, causing me to take a step back. It was as if she'd morphed into a firework, about to explode at any moment. She got to her feet and marched her way over to where Matt's wife, Sophia, and I still stood.

"Who are you?" Sophia asked, her voice hesitant.

"I'm Abigail, his fiancée! What happened to him?" she hollered as she stared us down. So this was who he was supposed to be proposing to on the beach that night instead of me. It seemed they did get engaged after all.

I took in the two females before me. One with long black hair and blue eyes. One with bright red hair and hazel eyes. Then there was me with my blond hair and hazel eyes. Matt wasn't just cheating on me with one person, but two other people? How did someone have the time to have all of these relationships and keep them a secret? What else what he keeping from us?

"Um, excuse me…" a voice said to my side. I turned to face the girl. She looked close to my age, but I would bet that I was at least a year or two older than her.

"Yes?" I answered. I wasn't sure what was going on, but it wouldn't hurt to hear the girl out, especially if she had information. Maybe she could clear the air about what was really going on here.

"I'm Charlotte.. Matt and I have been sleeping together..."

My lips pursed as Abagail exploded. It definitely did hurt to hear what she had to say, for she'd just added more confusion to the mix. On this mountain two hours away from the closest city, and days away from Florida, was a dead guy who just happened to be my ex, who was here with not only his wife, but his fiancée and some girl he had been sleeping with.

"Did you get all of that? Because I'm lost."

I nodded in reply to my best friend, for I too was lost.

# Chapter Three

The crowd was forced to disperse, but the employees of the lodge had requested all of us involved with Matt to stay present in the lodge area. The four ladies, including myself, that were involved with Matt were seated together at a table and it was the most awkward moment of my life—even topping the movement on the beach where I thought I was getting proposed to. Abigail shot daggers at everyone and every few moments would say something snarky. She still didn't believe any of us were involved with him, as she deemed us below average looking. Her exact words might have been: "If the bar was on the ground, you three went and brought a shovel." But who was really taking note of what spewed from the fiery red dragon's mouth? I certainty wasn't.

"I was told that the cops wouldn't be able to make it up the mountain due to the weather," Charlotte said as she brought her cup of water to her lips for a sip. Out of everyone, she was the calmest, but that might have been because she knew Matt the least. She didn't have as much as a history as, say, someone who had been married to the man for five years. My eyes darted over to his wife, who looked like she had been punched in the gut repeatedly. The smeared makeup didn't help.

"So why are we here, then?" Abigail asked as a man ventured into the lodge. He was a tall man with brown hair. His hand was wrapped around the straps of his messenger bag as he made his way over to us.

"Afternoon, ladies, I am Jared," he introduced himself as he laid his messenger bag on the table. Neither of us greeted him in return. In the short amount of time we were grouped together, I was sure everyone in the lodge would know our names by now.

After all, it wasn't every day you heard of a man who was involved with several women and wound up dead, especially on a mountain two hours away from the nearest city.

"I'll be questioning you all today."

"I thought the police couldn't make it up the mountain," Charlotte inquired.

"That is correct. They can't make it up the mountain, but I will enter the police academy next semester. So technically I will be a police officer."

My eyebrow raised at the man before me as I fully took him in. He wore slacks, and a white button-down shirt that was a few sizes too big for him. On top of his head was a pair of regular glasses. I wasn't sure why he was wearing them like sunglasses, but perhaps it was more of a fashion statement. But as I looked back down at his oversized shirt that spilled from his jeans at his attempt of tucking them in, I retracted my previous thought. I wasn't sure if he knew what fashion was.

"So why should I allow myself to be questioned by a wanna-be cop?"

Abigail didn't have a care in the world if she hurt someone's feelings. She truly not only had a fiery head of hair but also spat fire with her words.

"Because ... I will find the true culprit and solve this case."

Jared brought his finger up to push the rim of his glasses back, but all he did was poke himself in the nose. I stifled a laugh as he brought his hand up to push down his glasses before pushing them up.

"Right, who wants to go first?"

He picked up his messenger bag back up once more as he waited for one of us to speak up. I didn't want to go first. I really had no information to contribute. Matt had just happened to be here at the same ski resort as I, and that was the end of the story. As I scanned the table, it seemed it was the exact opposite, for all eyes were on me. I pointed to myself as if verbally asking if they wanted me to go first.

"Well, isn't it obvious you should go first?" Abigail said as I turned my attention to her.

"Why is that?" I countered.

"Because you're the ex."

"Right, then, will you follow me?" Jared said.

Jared motioned for me to follow him. I threw one last look around at the females at the table before letting out a sigh. There would be no point in arguing with them. The sooner we got this taken care of, the sooner I could put all of this behind me and truly enjoy my vacation. Jared walked into an office room that was behind the front desk of the lounge area. It seemed he had pulled some strings to be able to question us in private.

"Please sit." He motioned to the chair, and I obliged. Let the questioning begin.

"Brittany Williams, correct?" he asked as I sat up straighter in my chair, trying to peer at the piece of paper he had pulled from his messenger bag as he sat down.

"That is correct. How did you know that?"

"I'm about to enter the police academy. Figuring out people's identifies is a basic skill required," he answered, but I bet he just went to the front desk and asked for our documents. He was putting together his suspect list, and I was the very first one.

"Can you tell me the reason for your trip up to this resort? Especially since it is so far away from home..." He trailed off as he peered at me, a pen appearing in his hand as he tapped it against the desk, waiting for my answer. I wasn't sure if he was trying to look intimidating, but knowing he forgot he had his glasses on his head and poked himself in the face would be ingrained into my memory. There would be no chance I would feel intimidated by the man.

"Well, I just got out of a bad relationship and needed a vacation. So here I am," I said as I threw my arms up and motioned around the office.

"Right. It says you checked in with one Sophia Smith on Thursday, and today is Friday..." He trailed off again.

"That is correct."

"Hmm ... don't you think that is suspicious that you were the last to arrive, and now ... Matt Jones ends up dead?"

I stared at Jared as his tapping of the pen against the desk stopped. A smile started to form, as if he was happy that he might have stumped me.

"We broke up. I didn't know he was going to be here. It just happened we all ended up on this mountain together."

"Right ... and how long have you known the other females?"

"I met them tonight."

"Before or after the death of Matt?"

"After..."

"Right ... just checking. Why don't you tell me about your day here on this mountain, where there just happens to be you ex-boyfriend and his other lovers."

I wanted to groan out in frustration. What kind of interrogation was this? I thought they were supposed to question suspects to figure out who did it, not corner them till they confessed to doing something they didn't do. There was no way that Jared with his not-a-cop butt was going to get me to confess to having to do anything with Matt's death. I wanted nothing to do with him when we broke up. All I wanted to do was forget him; that was the whole reason I took this trip to this forsaken mountain. But if Jared wanted to play a game, I would at least play along so I could leave this room. I spilled everything that happened from the very moment Sophia and I arrived. Which wasn't much considering this was only our second day, but still everything was laid out on the table.

"Hmm ... very good ... and to confirm you knew of him dating another female?"

"That is correct. That is why we broke up," I answered.

"And you planned the trip and invited your friend along?"

"That is correct."

"And you just happened to pick the same mountain?"

"That is correct." I rolled my eyes. It was the same questions over and over just asked in a different way each time. There would be no plot holes in my story, for I had nothing to do with Matt's death.

"Right ... if you will excuse me for a moment," he said as he pushed back in his chair to stand before heading to the door to leave the office. I tracked his movements as he left the room, leaving the door slightly cracked. Still present at the table were the other females who were involved with Matt, waiting their turn to be questioned. But Jared's voice drew my attention away from the girls as I tried to see who he was talking to.

"Sir, I have solved the case. Yes, the evidence is clear as day. Yes, I will make sure she doesn't catch on. Yes sir, it's the ex-girlfriend..."

I brought my hand up to smack my face. Did I really just hear that? After all of this questioning and answering I did, I was still the suspect? What was the point of listening to me if he was just going to say it was me anyway? Especially since he hadn't heard the other women's stories yet, just mine. He had a lot of nerve casting me as the suspect to kill my ex-boyfriend. Yes, I had every reason to want him dead, but that didn't mean I had a hand in his death. I snorted as I thought of Jared more. He never said exactly where he would be going to the police academy. If he was going to be in my town, I would move. Better yet, he should not be allowed to even be a cop if this was the best he had to offer.

"Thank you for waiting," he said as he re-entered the room, and I raised my eyebrow in response. It was hard to take him seriously after everything I had just heard mere seconds ago.

"You are free to go, but please stay on the mountain," he said as he sat back down in his chair, clasping his hands together, a big smile on his face as if he were proud of himself for capturing the culprit, but he was far from the truth. If he thought I was the culprit, then I would deliver the real one on a silver platter to him. And just maybe, to add more salt to the wound, I'd go to the police academy instead of him.

# Chapter Four

"So my best friend is going to jail? There is a first for everything." Sophia spoke as if she wasn't fazed as she lounged on the bed in our shared room.

"I'm not going to jail."

"That's not what Jared thinks."

"I don't think you should be putting value to Jared's opinions."

"Oh, I don't, but who do you think the cops are going to listen to?" she asked as she sat up. "The ex-girlfriend of the dead guy or the guy going to the police academy?"

"Exactly!" I exclaimed as I crossed my arms over my chest. Her eyebrow raised at my outburst and I knew she was just waiting for more information on why I was so happy.

"We are going to solve this case."

"Who is we?" she countered.

"We as in us."

"Why do you keep including me in this we? That's how we got into this mess in the first place," she huffed.

"We took the vacation together, so shouldn't we solve the crime together?"

"No. Again, how does that even make sense in that mind of yours?"

I ignored her as I grabbed her arm and hauled her from the bed. We had an investigation to start and we wouldn't be able to get anything done if we stayed in our room the whole time. We needed to get out there in the thick of it to find the true culprit and clear my name.

"I don't like that look on your face. It spells trouble."

With my hand firmly on my best friend's arm, we made our way out of our room and down the hallway to the stairs so we could go back down to the lounge area. With the body removed from the deck, people went about enjoying their business. A few people stopped to turn to look at me as I passed, but I paid them no mind for I needed to stay focused on my goal. It wasn't communicated when the cops would be able to come up the mountain; the only thing prohibiting them was the weather. As of now, Mother Nature was on my side, allowing me time to solve the case, but all that could change with the shift of the wind, literally.

"So how are we going to solve this?" Sophia asked as I tugged her to the ledge to peer down into the lounge. None of Matt's other lovers were present, which was good. I couldn't have them getting suspicious of me while I was trying to prove one of them did it.

I was examining the room, trying to find a way to collect information, when a man walked out of the office that I was previously questioned in and hopped on the computer on the front desk. My mouth curved into a smile. He would be just the right person to talk to. I shifted away from the ledge to the stairs to start my descent down when a very familiar voice piped up. Instinctively, I dropped to the ground and dragged Sophia down with me.

"Shh!" I hissed as I watched Jared appear from the office as well. He shook the man's hand, adjusting his messenger bag and making his way over to the stairs.

To the very place I was hiding.

"I didn't say anything."

"Hide!" I whispered, as I crawled on the floor to avoid being seen from in between the beams of the ledge. I wanted to avoid running into the man who was about to be going to the police academy, for he would surely ask some more ridiculous questions. Which would only further make him believe I had something to do with Matt's death.

I found a supply closet that I could possibly hide in, wiggled the doorknob and, as if luck were on my side, it was unlocked. With no moment to waste, I threw the door open and crawled the rest of the way in before looking for Sophia, finding her still sat by the ledge looking at me with her eyebrows raised and a grin on her face. I let loose a sigh. I must have looked ridiculous. But nevertheless we were running out of time. If Sophia didn't haul it, we both would be caught. I motioned for her to come, but in return she crossed her arms.

"Come!" I whispered, doing my best to make sure she could hear me, but also that I wasn't too loud to draw additional attention to myself. Being in a supply closet on the ground while whispering loudly would surely cause anyone to give a second glance to figure out what was going on.

"Why? I didn't do anything," she bit back.

"'Cause you are here with someone who supposedly did something. So we need to hide."

"I'm getting tired of this 'we.' Why did I even come on this vacation?"

She let out a sigh, but obliged my request and crawled her way over to the supply closet just in the nick of time. As I was closing the door behind her, the top of Jared's head came into view. He wasn't looking our way, focused on the steps, so it allowed us to hide away without being seen. Now all we had to was wait for the coast to be clear and we could resume our investigation into who really had a hand in the Matt's death. I slumped against the wall, as all we could do was wait and hope Jared didn't linger.

"I can't wait to tell everyone back home about this," Sophia exclaimed as she sat down next to me in the small supply closet. I could make out her face from the light that seeped underneath the door, but it provided barely any help illuminating the rest of the closet to see what else was in here. I shifted as I leaned against the door, pressing my ear to the wood, trying to listen to what was happening outside. I couldn't hear Jared's voice, but that didn't mean he wasn't out there. I would need to look to see if the coast was clear. Opening the door was out of the question, for that would cause anyone nearby to look. And on the off chance they got spooked easily, they might scream if they saw a door being opened with no one nearby. Nope, I would need to press myself against the ground and try to look through the crack between the door and floor.

The things I must do to clear my name.

I pressed my face to the floor, doing my best to not think about the last time someone cleaned inside the supply closet, and with one eye scanned the area I could see. Which wasn't much because there wasn't a lot going on near the floor, but I could see several pairs of shoes.

"What are you doing?" Sophia asked as she shuffled next to me. A weight pressed against me as she used me as support to lean her ear against the door.

"Oh, now you're interested in solving the case?" I let loose a chuckle at her change of heart.

"Shh ... I'm trying to listen."

I rolled my eyes and continued to peer underneath the door, but my body froze as a pair of shoes were making their way right to the supply closet.

There is no way someone knows we are in here, right?

Jared had not seen us, so we should have been in clear. Yet, the lump in my throat grew as the pair of shoes stopped right in front of the door and blocked majority of the light. The doorknob twisted, and I wiggled, trying to get Sophia off me in case we needed to make a run for it, but it was no good. The supply closet door was yanked open and we came tumbling out. I looked up at the person who had opened the door and relief flooded through as it wasn't Jared, but it was quickly replaced with annoyance, for I knew the face.

"Why, it's the ex-girlfriend of the dead guy," the man said, his deep voice louder than I had wished. It was the man we had encountered in the crowd who had loudly exclaimed my relationship to the dead guy. The very same guy who was doing the same thing twice in one day and drawing too much attention to me.

"What are you doing in there?" he asked as he took a few steps back and crossed his arms.

"We don't owe you an explanation. You aren't a cop," Sophia countered as she untangled herself from me and stood to square off against the huge man.

"Should I go get the cop, then? I think his name was Jared."

"He isn't a cop either!"

Sophia grabbed my arm and pulled me from the floor.

"Where are you going?"

"Away from you! How did you even know we were in there? If anything, you are the suspicious one!"

The man's face morphed into shock as he brought a finger to point at himself. He was in disbelief at being called suspicious, but Sophia was right. How did he know we were in there? The man stayed at the top of the stairs as we made our way down them to the lodge's center. By the time we made it to the main floor, he was gone.

# Chapter Five

I watched every move of the front desk guy, waiting for an opening to approach. In order for me to gather information on the other females involved, I needed some type of information on them.

Fingers tapping against the table added a light distraction as I tried to stay focus on the task at hand. Sophia had gotten bored and decided to get another cup of hot apple cider and was currently tapping away on the table while enjoying her drink.

"When are you going to make your move?"

"Right now," I answered as I hopped out of my chair and headed to the front desk. He was finally alone, which was the perfect time to try to gather information from him.

"How can I help you?" he asked without missing a beat. He didn't look up as I approached, keeping his head down as he tapped away against the keyboard at intense speeds.

"I was wondering if I could have some records…"

His eyes darted up only briefly before focusing back on his keyboard. He provided no response, and I was about to ask again when he finally stopped typing. His eyes met mine and I smiled, hoping to make myself look as friendly as possible.

"Sorry, Mrs. Williams, I can't help you with any of your requests. Everything must go through Jared."

"Oh, it's just a tiny request though. I'm sure we don't need to bother Jared. After all, he is getting ready for the police academy."

"Sorry, ma'am, orders are orders," he said, turning around and fussing with something behind him. I wasn't sure if he was actually doing work or just trying to make it look like he was busy in hopes it would send me away. Either way, it worked, as I walked back to the table in defeat. The man hadn't even been willing to hear me out on why I needed records, and had just shot me down. I guess if a suspect in a death asked me for some records, I would shoot them down too.

"That was fast."

I answered my best friend with a huge huff as I slouched down in my seat. I needed another plan and needed it fast. I could not afford to dwell longer in the lounge in case Jared came back. Or even the man with the deep voice who kept popping up at the wrong times and talking loudly.

"Since you insist we are in this together, I'll handle it. Just wait for my signal?"

"What signal?" I asked, but she did not elaborate. She got up from her seat, apple cider in hand, and she made her way to the front desk. What kind of signal would she send? I didn't have to wait long. When she was a few feet away from the front desk, she tipped her hot apple cider onto the floor, and with no hesitation at all she walked right into in and did the most dramatic, non-Oscar worthy fall to the ground. If the man behind the front desk had been looking up from his keyboard, he would not have been fooled. But luck was on our side, for he was once more typing away, but the commotion caused by Sophia drew his attention immediately.

"Oh help! I seem to have fallen!" Sophia hollered as she gripped her left arm to her chest. She shot a few winks in my direction as the man behind the counter rushed out from behind his desk to assist my dramatic best friend. A snort escaped me at her antics as I made my way to the counter, doing my best to not look in her direction, lest I caught the eye of the employee and her performance would be all for nothing. I couldn't let this marvelous piece of acting go to waste, so I slinked behind the counter and started typing away. I didn't have anyone's full name except for Olivia, as she was Matt Jones' wife, so the chances of them sharing a last name was high. The chances of them booking together were even higher. With a quick search in the database, I found the records tied to one Olivia Jones, and with a little finger wag I pressed print.

My heart stopped as the printer in the office started to make a loud noise in preparation to print out my request. It would grab the employee's attention. Not even a second later, the man turned around, pausing in his attempt to aid my best friend to see what was going on. But speed was on my side. I ducked under the counter and waited. I didn't have to wait long. Sophia had heard the printer as well and let loose a very loud groan, followed by exclaiming, "It hurts!"

I peeked my head up from behind the counter to confirm the employee wasn't looking my way before continuing my search on the others. I didn't know Abigail's last name, but finding a picture of a fiery redhead with a face that could kill you with her glares would be easy. With just a few clicks, I had her profile pulled up, and just like before I hit print. But this time I ducked down immediately instead of waiting to see the employee assisting Sophia would inspect to see why something was printing.

Sophia let loose another howl of fake pain, and I snorted at her acting skills. I couldn't see her from behind the counter, but she was putting on the best show of her life. Only waiting a few moments, I popped back up and began typing away once more to locate the last individual, Olivia. It was a common name and all I could do was hope a thousand Olivias didn't pop up in the system and I would have to search through them all. But it seemed like someone out there wanted me to solve the case, as the exact Olivia I was looking for popped up as the first search result. She had a bright gold star next to her name, like someone had saved her booking, but I wasn't sure what that meant.

Whoever did that, though, I would have to thank them for making my job easier. With another few clicks, I had her files printing; I would be all set to start my investigation. I threw my body to the ground and crawled my way to the printer, swiping my prizes and hauling my butt from behind the counter and back into the lounge. I spared a quick glance Sophia's way to see how she was doing, and her eyes met mine. One moment she was clinging to the employee, her arm wrapped around his neck as she leaned on him, wailing, and the next moment she was saying she was all fine leaving the puzzled employee left behind.

"Got the goods?" she whispered.

"Yeah. By the way, why didn't you tell me you can act?" I countered, and all I got for my witty tongue was a glare. The employee that was once helping Sophia had migrated back behind the counter and was inspecting the printer, no doubt trying to figure out what was causing it to go off while he assisted some crazy lady. But too bad. I was just too sneaky. It also helped that Sophia was there. I turned my attention back to the stairs and made my way up to the floor we were staying on. It was time to study the evidence and clear my name.

"I'm hungry. I worked up an appetite with that scene you made me pull."

"If I remember correctly, it was you who had a plan. I never told you to do that."

"If I waited any longer to speak up, you would have had me doing something even more crazy. I know you."

"If you say so."

But she was right. I had no intention of going to jail, and especially having it be due to Matt Jones. He'd already humiliated me once. And for that to happen a second time? Over his dead body. Or mine ... since he was dead?

I shook the thoughts from my head as I climbed the last few steps to make it to our floor and headed right to our shared room. Sophia immediately picked up the phone to order some room service while I got to work. With a swipe of my arm across the table, the contents that once littered the surface now covered the floor. I would clean it up later, as I needed the space.

I picked up Olivia's paper first. It had information on both her and Matt because they had checked in together. A room with a single bed was booked, and they arrived on Sunday. As I continued to scan the papers, everything else was generic information. Nothing to really point to Olivia as the culprit. With a sigh, I set down her records and picked up Abigail's. My head reeled back as I processed the items on her record. She had arrived on Tuesday, which wasn't the alarming piece. No, the piece that had me gripping the papers tightly was the amount of money she was spending. A spa treatment twice a day, private lessons, and room service were just a few of the items listed on there. And with a spa treatment of three hundred, coupled with the fact it was twice a day, caused any bill to rapidly increased.

"What? You find what you are looking for?"

"She's rich?"

"Who Olivia?"

"No, Abigail."

"I'm not surprised, considering that attitude she has."

For someone who had only been here a few days, she'd racked up a bill in the thousands already. On her document, though, it showed, she'd checked into a single occupancy and not with Matt Jones. Olivia and Matt checking in together and then Abigail showing up later alone was looking awful suspicious. Hopefully even more so than myself where we can move Jared's sights from myself and onto the redhead.

It wouldn't be enough though. I needed more information. Another quick scan of Abigail's sheet had me wondering if she even had time to do anything alone or was everything on her itinerary the perfect alibi. A smirk formed on my face. But for good measure, I had one last suspect to review, Charlotte, who had a mysterious gold star next to her name.

I got to examining her information and was quickly puzzled. Her check-in date was several years ago. Did she live up here? It also had her room checked as the VIP penthouse. When I thought of penthouses, the only thing that came to mind were the ones that I had seen on TV. I didn't have the money to afford a penthouse, hence I had never set foot in one. But a penthouse suit in a cabin style lodge on a mountain two hours away from a city? That was odd, but not the oddest thing to happen here though. The more I examined Charlotte's paperwork, the more I thought she was just here at the wrong time and happened to bump into Matt. I was pretty sure Matt hadn't been to this mountain before or he would have mentioned it.

But again, I couldn't be too sure about the information he shared with me, considering he never mentioned he was married.

"So is it Charlotte, Abigail, or Olivia?"

# Chapter Six

**"Y**ou know, I don't think hot apple cider goes with every meal," I managed to say as I shoved another mouthful of noodle soup into my mouth. A shiver coursed through my body as the hot, flavorful liquid coupled with noodles got to work, creating magic in my mouth. I followed by picking up my bowl and bringing it to my lips as I drowned down some of the liquid.

"Who knew there would be such a wide range of variety on a mountain?" Sophia managed to blurt as she alternated taking bites and drinking from her hot apple cider. "And by the way, don't diss the hot apple cider. That is how you got me on this trip in the first place."

"I thought it was because we are best friends," I said as I acted like I was hurt by her assertions.

"That's reason number two. Reason number one is because of this deliciousness."

For good measure, she raised her glass and swirled it around for a moment before taking a long gulp and letting out a satisfied ahh. I rolled my eyes at her antics. I would say ever since her display in the lodge, she had been riding the high of her short-lived acting career.

"Are you ready to get back to investigating?"

"We just had dinner, we are supposed to relax. Why are we going back to work?"

"Well, it's either we get back to work or I get ready to go to jail," I countered.

"You make it sound like it's a bad thing."

"It's not something I really want to find out."

I got up from my seat at the table. The documents were neatly tucked away to avoid the chances of any liquid staining them from slurping the noodle soup. With my bowl in hand, I grabbed Sophia's bowl and stacked them on the tray the food arrived on. The instructions were to leave the tray outside the door and room service would come by and pick them up, so that is exactly what I did. Sophia soon joined me in the hallway and we were on our way to continue our investigation. I still had some questions regarding who exactly Charlotte was, but I was sure her connection with Matt was short lived, especially since he died. Abigail, though, was a whole different story. She knew Matt prior to arriving on this mountain; after all they were engaged and she arrived on this mountain alone, where Matt was already here with his wife. If that didn't ring alarm bells, I wasn't sure what did.

"Who are we looking for?" Sophia asked as she trailed behind me.

"Abigail first."

"Ah yes, let's go look for the person who might have a hand in the death of your ex-boyfriend."

"I thought you were on board," I said.

"I am. But I just wanted to let you know this is probably a bad idea."

I made my way down the stairs and out to the deck, where the bonfires were. The slopes were closed for the night, so everyone would find other ways to occupy their time, and sitting around a fire pit was the best thing to do. I scanned the area of the deck to see if I could find my target, but her fiery red hair was nowhere to be found. But instead of red hair, I did find two women, one with black hair and one with blond. How odd that Olivia and Charlotte would be sitting together. They weren't my prime suspects, but them hanging out was starting to make it seem like I might be wrong.

"Keep a lookout and let me know if you see Abigail," I whispered to Sophia as I crouched to the floor.

"What kind of signal?"

"Are you seriously asking me that after that display you did earlier?" I questioned.

"It was a once in a lifetime acting, don't expect the same performance."

"Anything will do."

I grabbed the empty chair in front of me and moved it a bit closer to the women as I hid behind it. The occupants of the fire pit stared at me, but I tried to not focus on them. I might look crazy, but I was a girl on a mission.

The chair screeched against the deck and I dropped to the floor. Briefly Charlotte looked over in our direction. As I peered out from underneath the chair, I waited till they got engaged back in their conversation once more before making a bolt to a huge flowerpot. A moving chair would soon draw too much attention, so something more subtle was needed. Like a giant flowerpot that was bigger than me. I was close enough that I could pick up words, but it was hard to put together. From my limited hearing, they discussed muffins, the beach, and the weather. I poked my head into the flowers, trying to bring my ear as close to them. I needed more information. They could be using code after all.

"KWAH KWAH!"

I gripped the flowerpot, poking my whole head through now to try to finally get a better understanding of what they were saying. A few people stared at me, but I was coming to terms that maybe it wasn't just Sophia who was crazy. We both were, and that might be why we became good friends in the first place.

"I SAID KWAH KWAH!" the voice screeched, and this time I turned around to see what had caused Sophia to put on such a horrible acting job. My mouth dropped as my body hit the floor once more. There was a redhead shooting dirty looks at Sophia, who was trying to act normal like she wasn't just screeching like a bird a moment ago. Abigail made her way over to Charlotte and Olivia, but in order to do so, she would have to pass me. My heart pounded in my chest. Where could I hide so I wouldn't be caught?

"Why are you in the flowerpot?" a man said as he stepped into view, effectively blocking me from Abigail. My hand flew to my chest, a heavy sigh released, for I had evaded being caught for the moment. I took in the figure who had decided to approach me, the familiar face of the man who either had the luckiest or the worst timing, depending on which side you looked at it. His deep voice was something I should ingrain in my memory, for we always seemed to be bumping into each other.

"You know you are the definition of suspicious," he said, crossing his arms across his chest as he looked down at me.

"And you are the definition of a stalker," I countered, crossing my own arms across my chest. I wouldn't look big or intimidating; it was more in a mocking way.

"Wait ... that's not what is going on. I'm just trying to make sure you aren't up to any funny business," the man said as he waved his hands in the air, trying to dismiss the tension between us.

"I'll look past this incident and won't speak about you being a stalker if you leave me be."

He stood there for a moment, looking down at me before letting loose a huge sigh. Hanging his head in defeat, he turned on his heels and left.

I slid from my position to peer around the flowerpot, still keeping my body close to the floor. I didn't want to risk looking through the flower once more, just in case Abigail was looking this way. Olivia was the only one seated now; both Abigail and Charlotte stood around the fire pit. I raised my eyebrows as I examined the girls. I had thought we didn't know of each other prior, but the way they easily talked to each other told a different story. My suspicion of being set up as the culprit in Matt's death was becoming even more clear. I was the odd woman out, and one of them, even maybe all three of them, were in on it.

"I have to go. It was nice catching up with you both!" Charlotte exclaimed as she leaned in to hug Abigail, waved a goodbye to Olivia, and turned on her heel to walk away. Thankfully, she wasn't heading back inside where she would have to pass by me, opting instead to walk further down the deck to someplace else. Something I added to my to do list: figure out where she went. I refocused my attention on Abigail, who now took a seat next to Olivia. It was quiet for a moment, and it allowed me to crawl forward slightly, to hide behind a row of chairs and a fire pit. They might be able to spot me if they looked close enough, but they shouldn't be looking down on the floor.

"I'm devastated he is gone," Olivia started.

"I know. It's crazy to think he was here one moment and gone the next," Abigail said as she leaned back in her chair, getting comfy. For someone who was still emotionally attached to Matt at the time of his death, she sure did have a calm demeanor. Maybe she just didn't grieve like most people. Couldn't hold her to it, but she was still my suspect number one.

"How did we all end up on this mountain together?"

"Yes, how did we?" I mumbled to myself. That was the key thing that needed to be solved. Why did we all venture to this one resort hours away from civilization? There were a bunch of resorts to pick from yet we all managed to arrive at the same one.

"Matt had mentioned he wanted to go to this mountain for a trip," Abigail said. "Work called and he got busy, so I decided to go to spite him for putting work first all the time." I rolled my eyes at her response. That seemed like an Abigail type of thing to do. I hadn't known the girl long, but she didn't seem like the type of person who let people mess with her. If she wanted something, she went after it. Even if it meant doing something out of spite. My eyes narrowed. Did she know Olivia and Matt were already here and that was why she came up here at this exact time? Upset that he took a vacation with his wife and not her?

"He sure did love his work. I wish I could have helped him out more with it."

"Trust me, you don't. That's thousands of dollars I won't be getting back," Abigail answered, as she threw her hands behind her neck. Alarms bell went off at her words. A red flag appearing on top of her head as it swung wildly in the air. Money could motivate anyone to do anything. If she had sunk money into Matt's failed business endeavors, that was enough to send anyone over the edge.

Matt was an odd one. He was a sweet talker, he could convince anyone with his compliments. That's how he got away with dating all of us at once. It would have been impossible if he didn't know how to lay it on thick and make the person feel like the most important person in the world. He was always talking about a business idea that would allow him to make millions where we could retire to an island and live our best life was his promise. Only one I half believed. After all, who wouldn't want to dream of the best future with the person they loved? All that was dashed though the night of the proposal, when it wasn't me he meant to marry. It was all a scam, and thank goodness I didn't have any money to invest in the million ideas he had, or Abigail and my positions might have been switched.

# Chapter Seven

A new day meant another day of following around after our suspects, namely Abigail. I had my sights set on her as target number one. Everyone else was a bonus. Of course, I would spend the time clearing their names. I couldn't blindly just go after the redhead no matter how much I wanted to. My gut was telling me that I was right. I also needed to wrap this up before the weather got better and Jared got on his high horse once more and the soon-to-be police academy student sent me off to jail for something I didn't do.

I downed my hot apple cider as I sat in the lounge. A strong addiction to the hot sweet liquid was developing, and I had Sophia to blame. Today, we would be observing, and I did my best to blend in with the crowd, a loose hat on my head that allowed me to tuck most of my hair up in it. At first glance, most wouldn't put me together with being the dead man's ex-girlfriend. To help the look even more, I had a huge pair of goggles on my head, but instead of sitting directly on top of my head, it covered my forehead and stopped right before my eyes. But that wasn't it. The scarf wrapped around my neck was puffed out to cover part of my nose and everything below. Which left really only my eyes to be exposed. My lips curved into a smile. This was a good disguise if I had to say so myself. It would look a little suspicious if I lingered too long in the lobby, but people would just assume I was about to hit the slopes. Which had re-opened despite a death happening on the mountain. The nearby town might be experiencing bad weather that it made it hard to make the long drive up the mountain, but people were here on vacation. A dead body wasn't going to stop them from enjoying their time off, so back outside they went.

I slouched in my seat as I waited for one of my targets to arrive in the lobby. There was no information on the girls about whether they were early birds or night owls. Which was how I found myself sitting in the lounge alone at the crack of dawn. I had tried to wake my roommate for the trip, but received a pillow to the face as she curled herself further into her blankets. Sophia was everything but a morning person.

My prayers were answered as a mop of blond hair descended the stairs and into the lobby. She headed straight to the front desk as I slouched further into my seat, trying to do my best to blend into the background. I had faith in my disguise, but one couldn't be too careful.

With a quick disappearance behind the front desk into the office, she reemerged with a stack of papers. Charlotte made her way over to an empty table in the lobby and placed her papers on the desk. But she didn't stay, for she turned and walked away. I tracked her movements, watching her weave her way through the lobby furniture to stand in line for food.

One should never leave their items unattended. You never know for who might be watching. In this case, it was me. I was watching.

I slid out of my seat and tried to walk as nonchalantly as possible to her table, my head on a swivel, trying to identify anyone who might be watching me.

With purpose in my step, I made my way over to her table, but I didn't sit down. Instead, I pretended to mess with my pockets, acting as if I was looking for something as I glanced down at the papers. If I pulled this off without getting caught, I was going to teach Sophia how to not draw attention with her over-the-top acting. Just in case we had to do this again.

The first page was a ledger, and upon straining my neck I saw it was a list of bills, itemizing electricity, water, food and a bunch of other services the resort needed to function. I took a cautionary glance around. Charlotte was paying at the counter, so I would only have moments before I had to scatter or risk capture. I swiped at the papers, taking a glance at what lay below the ledger sheet. A defeated sigh escaped, for it just went into more detail about the costs, and an itemized list of things ordered for the restaurant, which showed a ridiculous amount spent on apple cider. I guess Sophia and I weren't the only ones becoming obsessed with the hot drink. With a quick stacking of the papers back into a neat pile, I made my way over to my table to further observe Charlotte.

Timing was on my side. Just as I sat down, she received her food and was on her way back to her table, none the wiser that I had a quick look through her papers.

Minutes turned into hours as Charlotte made no motion to get up from her table, opting instead to continue scribbling away on her papers. Was she seriously working on financial information this whole time? My face scrunched up as I leaned farther back in my seat. My body was getting stiff from just sitting here. I was also immensely bored watching someone content with just writing and doing nothing else. Don't think I had even heard her utter a word. I pushed out of my seat throwing my arms over my head as I did some stretches. Needed to get the blood flowing through my body once more or I might end up dead like Matt next.

A small chuckle escaped, for if I also ended up dead, that would derail Jared's whole investigation. He was dead set on me being the culprit, but if the culprit dies, then who truly is the one pulling the strings?

"Working on the finances?" a lodge employee asked as he made his way up to join Charlotte at her desk. It was the same man who had been the victim of Sophia's horrible acting when she had fallen in the lobby. I wondered what he had thought about that whole display. Was it worthy of an Oscar?

"Of course. Got to get this done or Father will be mad," she grumbled as she finally set her pen down on the table, leaning back in her chair in the process. My eyebrows raised, as my curiosity was piqued, for it was time to finally learn something about Charlotte. After sitting here for hours, I would take any information about the girl, even if it was just about her father. I settled once more into my seat, crossing my legs and slouching forward. At a glance, I would look like just a normal tourist who had fallen asleep in the lobby. Or that was at least what I hoped I looked like.

"Business has been booming lately. All thanks to you."

"Well, if I want to inherit this place, I got to keep it in working order."

"I bet your father is happy he banished you to the mountainside."

"He didn't banish me. I chose this life."

"Right ... let me know if you need me. I got a few things to take care of," the employee said, excusing himself from the table and walking off. Their exchange had my mind reeling.

Matt had a thing for girls with money, it seemed. Abigail had money, and now Charlotte had been identified as someone having money. She had plans to inherit this whole resort up here on the mountain. Surely that wasn't cheap. I stroked my chin as I tried to connect the dots. Olivia didn't seem to come from money. She couldn't invest in Matt's businesses, yet they were married. But they also had been together the longest. Everyone else, including myself, were side pieces. Since I didn't have money like Abigail, that was probably why he proposed to her and not me. Thankfully, being just an average person who wasn't sitting on a fountain of wealth had come in handy.

"Brittany, what are you doing? Why do you look like that?" a very familiar voice said.

I looked up into the face of my best friend. I lunged out of my seat, grabbing a hold of her arm and jerking her down into a seat. She had spoken too loud and it would draw attention.

"Why didn't you wake me up? Half the day is already gone," she said, bringing a cup up to her lips to sip from. If I had to take a guess, it was hot apple cider.

"I did try. You hit me with a pillow," I hissed.

"I thought that was a dream..." she mumbled.

"Brittany?"

"Yes?" I answered immediately, as I jerked to the new voice to join us. Charlotte had gotten up from her seat and walked over to our table, papers in hand. Without waiting for an invitation, she invited herself to sit down with us.

"Oh..." Sophia whispered as she looked from Charlotte to me. I rolled my eyes, oh indeed.

"Did the both of you just wake up?" Charlotte inquired.

"Sure did. I'm going to excuse myself to go do … something," Sophia said as she pushed out of her seat and hightailed it out of here. Straight out of the mess she had caused. I let loose a groan. I had gone a decent amount of time at not being noticed and Sophia had ruined it all within a moment. Of course she would be able to spot me. We were best friends, so even covered from head to toe she would still be able to identify me. But that didn't mean point it out in a lobby with other people, especially someone I'm trying to find information out on.

"How are you doing today?"

"Fine. Sorry if it seems I'm being nosy, but I couldn't help but catch the last bit of your conversation with that dude. Your father owns this place?" I pressed, trying to make it sound like I was simply curious and not prodding to see if she was Matt's murderer.

"Yeah, dad is a real business tycoon. This is just one of the many businesses he acquired."

"Oh, so that makes you rich, then."

"By association, yeah. I don't really have a need to spend money though. I live on this mountain full time."

When we had pulled the documents from the computer, that was why it was hard to determine how long she would be staying here. It was because she actually lived here up on this mountain!

"So you never leave the mountain?"

"No need. Everything I need is up here."

I was pretty sure there wasn't a dentist office up here, but I guess when you had money, maybe the medical people traveled to you instead of the other way around. I nodded, playing along. Being stuck on this mountain didn't seem very fun. There was only so much you could do in one spot. Charlotte was an odd one, but I didn't think she had anything to do with Matt's death. She had money and wanted to inherit the lodge, and if she got convicted of a crime, all that would be in jeopardy. Might as well ask her about her relationship with Matt. She was being an open book today, sharing all of her information. It was best to get it from the source, after all.

"So you and Matt..." I started, hoping she got the hint and would take over.

"Just a fling. Nothing more than that," she answered, and I wanted to ask another question but she continued on. "I like to think of myself as Rapunzel, except I'm not looking for a prince."

I stared at the girl before me. Charlotte might be weird, but being weird didn't mean she was involved.

"Just to let you know, I don't think you had anything to do with it. I think it was actually the wife."

I leaned forward. Was there information she was privy to that I hadn't found out yet? Maybe sitting down with the future owner of the lodge had worked out in my favor. Hit two birds with one stone. Not only did I get information on Charlotte, courtesy of herself, I was about to get information on Olivia.

"Why do you think that?"

"It's always the wife in the movies," she answered in a matter-of-fact tone, like there was nothing wrong with what she said, leaving me dumbfounded. Not only did we have a wannabe cop on the mountain accusing me of being the culprit, we had someone predicting guilt or innocence based on the plot of cliched movies. This investigation was going as smooth as a jagged rock.

# Chapter Eight

I left Charlotte at the table to do her work. The information I acquired was useful to a point. It confirmed my thinking that she really had no motive to have a hand in Matt's death. Why kill someone on her mountain when it might ruin the reputation of her business, which could result in its closing? No, she had personally chosen to make the mountain her new home.

There just wasn't a solid reason for her to care what Matt did. She wasn't looking for a prince. Once Matt left the mountain that would have been the end of their relationship.

Olivia, on the other hand, was the most likely suspect according to Charlotte, who consumed too many movies. I didn't want to rule Olivia out just because the wife is oftentimes the one who commits the crime. It could have been Abigail. The fiancée scorned who had lost money due to Matt's horrible business endeavors was the perfect back story to commit a crime that resulted in his death.

"You have the worst timing," I grumbled as I joined Sophia at the table she squirreled away at after blowing my cover.

"I can see that. Sorry about that. What did you learn?"

"I don't think it's Charlotte. She really has no reason to do it."

"Still stuck on Abigail?"

"It has to be, unless someone else is at play that we aren't factoring in."

"It's real life, not a murder mystery," Sophia countered as she chugged the last of her apple cider. She got out of her seat and I helped her clean off the table from her breakfast before heading outside.

"Do you think we have time to hit the slopes for a few? All this work is exhausting. It's supposed to be a vacation."

I stared at my best friend. Her definition of working was obviously different from mine. She had slept in today and had only just woken up. So far in the investigation the majority of the work she had done had consisted of falling to the ground, making bird noises, or blowing my cover. She was having fun and I was the one working.

"Why are you looking at me like that?"

"Like what?" I countered. I guess my face was too obviously pointing out that there was really only one person working among us.

"What a surprise, seeing you ladies out and about, especially you, Brittany," a very familiar voice spoke up from behind us. I let out an audible groan. It was hard to forget the voice of the man who was trying to send me to jail for a crime I didn't commit. I turned around to look at Jared, our very own soon-to-be police academy student who thought he was already a police officer. A smirk was plastered on his face as he brought his arms up to chest.

"Returning to the scene of the crime? Is there something you are trying to hide?"

His tone was getting on my nerves. Like he had figured out the biggest secret in the world, yet he was blindly charging down the wrong path and not investigating anyone else. Even though I had my suspicions of Abigail, I still made sure to gather information on Olivia and Charlotte. If anyone should be going to the police academy, it should me. I obviously had put more effort into actually solving this case than him.

But being a police officer was not my dream.

"No, we were actually thinking about going to the slopes," Sophia interjected, helping to release some of the tension that was growing the longer I looked at Jared's face.

"Do you think it is wise to go out there?"

I narrowed my eyes at the man. I caught the hint laced in his words. It was a two point jab, one at Sophia for going out to the slopes with someone who potentially had something to do with Matt's death—but I didn't. The other was towards me. The way his eyebrows furrowed gave me the impression he thought I might try doing something drastic, like run. Trying to hike down a mountain that took two hours by wheels wasn't exactly the speediest of escapes. Someone had to be completely crazy if they thought this mountain was walkable, and even crazier to attempt it. Jared did have a few loose screws, so I guess anything was possible in his mind.

"I haven't seen you around the lodge lately ... it's been quiet," Jared chimed in once more. I set the man with a stare. We lived in different worlds. I had been truly trying to investigate the crime. He would have noticed if he had been doing his job as well, and doing surveillance. I was also sure Sophia's acting out was anything but quiet. If he had seen the scene in the lobby, her on the ground holding on to the employee, wailing loudly, he would have had a change of mind.

"I have been around," I answered.

"Yes, I think it would be best you don't go out to the slopes. We need to have you within grasp after all. I shall tell the front desk to revoke your slope privileges."

It wasn't like he was asking my opinion on something, more along the lines of voicing his thoughts. He turned on his heels and walked inside without a moment's hesitation, certainly not waiting for any further comments from me.

"I'm not a big of fan of him."

"Join the club," I replied to my best friend as I watched Jared shuffle through the furniture and around people lingering in the lobby, making his way to the front desk to talk to the same employee who had sat down with Charlotte when she went over budgets. I threw a lingering look over my shoulder to the slopes that were now forbidden to me. It would seem I would be confined to the lodge till this case could be solved. With no other reason to be outside, I headed back inside, Sophia at my heels as we made our way to the stairs to go up to our rooms.

"Let's stop by Abigail's room to see if she is in before the lodge police decides to take away my privileges of talking to people as well."

Sophia let loose a chuckle as we made our way up the stairs. After a quick stop at Abigail's room, I would retreat back to my room to plot my next moves. Which would consist of now avoiding Jared as number one and with number two getting the real culprit captured.

"Isn't that her room?" Sophia said up as she pointed to an open door fast approaching. As we got closer, a heavy feeling settled in my chest. It grew heavier as I stood in the open door of the redhead's room. It was like a tornado had come through, breaking items and casting them to the floor. Whoever did this would have a huge bill to pay to the lodge for the damages to their property: table and chairs cracked on the floor, the lamp that usually sat on the table now shattered, the sheets in a heap and clothes thrown about. I wasn't sure if someone just went through a fit of rage or something far darker had happened. I stepped into the room, being careful to not mess with the evidence. Being here already was bad enough. I didn't need to have my fingerprints all over items as well.

"I wonder what happened in here," Sophia said, grabbing my attention. She had a stack of papers in her hands as she sat on the bed. I didn't know I needed to tell her to not put her fingerprints everywhere, but it was too late. The damage was done. A heavy sigh escaped. It was more fuel for Jared to think I had a hand in Matt's death—and now whatever had happened to Abigail—if he ever found out we were in here.

Time couldn't be rolled back, so I inspected the room, trying to identify what had really unfolded. Everything was scattered on the floor, things gone through, but no blood or any real sign that a fight had happened here. More like someone was searching for something but didn't find what they were looking for. I pressed on, looking under the bed, to see if anything got swept underneath there, but nothing other than a few garments of clothing.

I looked out the window, a bright red capturing my attention, and upon focusing I saw it was a mop of red hair. It trailed behind a mop of black hair as I moved closer to the window to look at the two people outside. That color of red wasn't that common with the tourists up here. The tingly feeling in the back of my brain was trying to tell me it was Abigail, but I needed confirmation. As if she could read my mind, the redhead tossed a look over her shoulder, spinning wildly trying to locate something. My eyes widened, as she had a piece of cloth stuck in her mouth. The mop of black hair turned, tugging on something, a piece of string by the looks of it. Not even a moment later, Abigail lurched forward, the piece of string wound around her wrists. I took in the face on the other end of the string—the culprit holding Abigail hostage. It was Olivia. She was the mastermind behind everything!

I hurled myself towards the door of Abigail's room so I could stop whatever was about to unfold from happening, only managing to get my words out in a jumbled mess to Sophia that we had to go. She jumped up from the bed, running after me, and we sprinted down the hallway towards the stairs.

My luck had ran out though. I screeched to a halt. Jared was walking up the last step to put him on the same floor as us, his eyes bulging as he raised his hand to point at us. I could see his eye dart from me and the room with the open door we had just ran out of. The gears were spinning in his head, no doubt, but I didn't have time to explain. I pushed past him, running down the stairs as I cast a look over my shoulder. He was only frozen for a moment before he took off in the direction of

Abigail's room. A slew of curses flew from my lips. If Jared had any thought that I didn't have a hand in Matt's death, that had just gone out the window. With the added pressure, I lit a fire under my feet. I had a culprit to catch before Jared got a hold of me.

# Chapter Nine

The lobby was a blur as I rushed through, weaving through the people standing about wanting an escape from the cold. Time was not on my side. Olivia and Abigail could have been long gone already. They had been out of my sight too long and I needed to get outside as soon as possible to pick up on their trail. Abigail was in trouble and despite her being a ball of bluntness, I didn't want something bad to happen to her. She'd just became the most important person in my life. She was my alibi. I needed to secure her future in order to secure mine. Our fates were now tied.

I rushed along the deck and down the stairs, sinking slightly into the snow as I went around the lodge to the location I had last seen the two women. Adrenaline coursed through my body, a tightness in my chest as I finally arrived where I had last seen them but they were nowhere in sight.

I looked to the ground. There were several sets of footprints scattered about on this side of the lodge. A slew of curses flew from my lips again as I crouched, inspecting the footprints. But I gave up pretty fast. I had no idea what type of shoeprint would come from their shoes, let alone how to read footprints enough to help me track them. I looked around wildly, trying to see if I could find any mop of red hair in all the snow. Nothing was standing out.

I could not afford to spend more time out here without having a clue to follow.

A heavy sigh escaped as I looked at the footprints once more. It was the only thing that could help me, and I needed to learn fast. I needed to channel my inner tracker in order to find Abigail before she ended up like Matt. Once more I crouched, inspecting the surrounding footprints. The first set of prints I ruled out were mine. I wasn't the suspect, no matter how much Jared wanted it to be me. Next, I ruled out any footprints that didn't have at least two different tracks. Which left three sets of footprints with promise.

The first went off deeper into the trees. My lips curved into a frown. Would they really go into the trees? If Abigail managed to loosen any of her restraints, she would be able to hide within the trees and escape. It was possible, but it was also unlikely. The last two sets of footprints headed in the direction of the slopes, so I followed them. My chances of being right were sixty-six percent, very good odds for someone who had never examined footprints before. My feet went on autopilot as I followed the prints, my head on a swivel, trying to find anything that was alarming.

"Brittany! Did you find them?" Sophia yelled as she came into view waving wildly, trying to get my attention.

"No!" I called back to the girl, but with another person here I didn't have to choose which track of footprints to follow. We each could follow one set. The only issue was one of us would encounter Olivia. She had already killed before and she was about to do it again. I gulped as I looked at my friend, who came to a halt beside me. When it was just solving the crime in the lodge with other people, I didn't think of the risks. But now it was the two of us about to go our separate ways after a killer. Could I ask her to do this? Put her life on the line and follow after a killer alone to clear my name?

"What's wrong?"

I bit my lip, as I didn't have time to mull over this. Abigail's time was running out. We needed to find her. With my resolve in place, I let out a heavy sigh.

"I need you to follow one set of tracks while I follow the other."

"Okay, which set?" Sophia asked as she looked to the ground.

"Just follow, and if you see Olivia, get help, okay? Neither of us need to wind up dead."

Sophia looked at me, arching her eyebrow in the process. We stared at each other for a moment before she let a laugh escape.

"Dying is not on my to-do list. Don't worry!"

Her smile calmed my nerves slightly, but worry for my friend would always be in the back of my mind. But there was some comfort that if Sophia managed to run into Olivia, she could put on the most dramatic show possible in order to gather a crowd. She would hopefully be safe.

Now all I had to worry about was making sure I stayed safe.

"You take the footprints to the left, and I'll go right."

Sophia nodded, taking off following the trail she was assigned. I watched her for a few seconds before following after my trail. The path my friend would follow would take her closer to the ski lifts. I wasn't exactly sure where mine would take me, only that it was still near the lodge.

I kept my eyes peeled for Amelia and her red hair as I walked in the snow. The tracks led me on a path away from the lifts, around the lodge and down a small hill. With my hands stuffed into the pockets of my coat, I tried my best to stay warm, but the temperature was dropping. If Abigail wasn't found soon, I might freeze out here. Despite being bundled up, the Florida in me was showing. A shiver coursed through my body as I picked up my speed.

Through the trees up ahead, a building could be seen. My heart pounded as there would finally be something other than footprints to stare at! Paneling a pale blue color with rust was clearly evident. My nose scrunched up. Either this building would tumble down, or one wrong touch and I would end up sick. Having a rusty nail go through any part of me was not on my bucket list. The footprints disappeared beyond the cracked door.

My stomach was roiling as I gripped the metal door, pulling it slightly to the side so I could at least poke my head through. A single light bulb swung slowly inside, casting the shed in a dim light. My hand shook, and I swallowed the lump forming in the back of my throat, for there wasn't a single moment the entire shed was basked in light; one side was always shrouded in darkness. With a hesitant step inside, I kept my eyes peeled and ears on high alert for any sort of movement that might indicate I wasn't alone out here. With my back to the wall, I scooted along the outskirt of the small building. It was one less place to be cautious of.

The light continued to swing. The pounding in my head forming as the pounding of my heart beat out of control. There was no way I was going to the police academy. Jared could keep that position. If I had to solve cases on the regular, I would give up. This would be my first and last case. After this, I was throwing in the towel and enjoying my vacation.

I froze as a groan echoed in the room, my gaze darting around trying to find who was in the room with me. I held my breath, waiting for another groan—but really I didn't want them to hear my heavy breathing and find me first. Several moments passed before I mustered up the courage to once more explore the shed. Like before, my back firmly pressed into the wall behind me, a bit harder this time. I sidestepped my way to the corner of the building, the light still swinging.

My foot knocked into something. The light swung away. I had to wait for it to swing back before I could look to see what blocked my progress. As the light highlighted my area in light, I cast my gaze down to the ground.

A scream ripped from my throat as I scrambled back towards the door. I tripped over my own feet in the process, sending me tumbling to the ground. The sight of a body on the ground was too much to handle. Bile rose in the back of my throat, threatening to escape as I crawled to the door. Only the legs were visible under the tarp that laid on top of the body, but it was too much. Tears spilled freely as I crawled away.

"Mmmmm!"

I froze as I slowly looked over my shoulder. The body under the tarp was wiggling. I clamped my hand over my mouth to muffle my scream. It only added fuel to the fire, for the body kept wiggling, its groans growing louder as it jerked about.

The person under the tarp wasn't dead. With my heart no longer beating out of control, but still loud enough to cause my head to pound, I made my way over to the body. With a huge gulp, I ripped the tarp off and stared at the person on the floor, who looked to be extremely pissed, and I was glad I wasn't the person who had made her so upset. I gripped the cloth in her mouth and tugged it down.

"Finally! What took you so long?" Abigail hollered as she wiggled, trying to sit up. I stared at her. She wouldn't be able to sit up on her own without help. Rope was tied tightly around her wrists and ankles.

"Honestly, I thought you were the crazy one! But Olivia is crazy too?"

I could see Abigail needed help, but I was content with just watching her. How could she still consider me crazy? I wasn't the one who bound her and left her in a shed to die.

"Are you going to untie me?"

I released a huge sigh at her shouts. Maybe it would have been best to leave her mouth gagged.

"Oh great. What do you want now?"

"What are you talking about?" I replied as I got to work freeing Abigail's hands.

"I'm not talking to you!"

If she wasn't talking to me, then who was she talking to? My fingers stopped working on untying the string, freezing in place as I whirled around to look behind me and stare up at Olivia, who had a shovel raised. I felt my eyes bulging as she swung. One moment there was light and the next all there was darkness. And pain. A lot of pain.

# Chapter Ten

There was a throbbing pain in my head. But the most annoying thing was that my mouth was itchy. I groaned as I tried to grasp whatever was in my mouth so I could remove it. My eyes shot open as my arms didn't budge from behind my back. Examining my surroundings, I took in the rusty pale blue shed, the events flooding back as someone shifted next to me.

With a glance over to see Abigail once more bound and gagged, I let out a huge groan, the itchy feeling increasing with my attempt to be audible.

Olivia had got the jump on me, and now both Abigail and I were bound in a shed. If the redhead wasn't such a loud person, we might have been able to escape. But I was sure her screams of displeasure at being roughly handled had brought Olivia scurrying back.

"Mmmmmm!" Abigail mumbled as I shot her a look. Was she mad at me for being captured? She was technically the first person that was caught. If anyone should be mad, it should be me.

"How did you know it was me?"

I rolled over so I could look in the direction of where the voice had come from. Olivia stood pacing in front of the door that led to the outside, blocking any chance of sweet freedom. That was if I managed to slip out of my imprisonment.

"Everything was going according to plan until now!"

Olivia fisted her hair, her pacing becoming more erratic. There was nothing I could do except watch her. I had been worried that Sophia would be the one to run into Olivia when I should have been more worried about myself. Abigail was still fidgeting beside me, but I didn't know what she wanted me to do. We were both bound and gagged.

Now it was just a waiting game to see what Olivia's next move would be. Hopefully, it wouldn't be killing either one of us. Or if it was, all I could hope for was that Abigail would be first.

"I don't understand … I don't understand…"

It was like listening to a mad woman talk to herself. Olivia stopped her pacing, standing still as she stared at us. I stared back to see what she would be doing next.

"I need to make a phone call," she mumbled as she ran outside. That was certainly not what I was expecting. Not sure who she needed to call at a moment like this, but whoever it was had just bought us some time. I rolled back over so I would be facing Abigail and I nudged my head to her. She stared for a moment before getting my signal and scooted my way. With her hands still tied behind her back, she tugged at the gag in my mouth as I jerked my head. The combined movement allowed the gag to fall out and free my mouth. I let loose a huge sigh of relief at having the itchy feeling go away. Abigail bobbed her head, drawing my attention.

"No, you make too much noise."

She groaned, bouncing up and down as best as she could in her predicament spent. It wasn't just Olivia that had made her upset, I was also now on that list.

Hopefully, she would be able to forgive me once we escaped this situation. If we escaped.

I rolled back over to face the door as I scooted back into Abigail. I shoved my hands as best as I could into her.

"Mmmm!"

"Untie me so we can escape."

"Mmmmm!"

"Fine, don't untie me and we will just wait for the crazy killer to come back."

I didn't need to be able to see Abigail to know what she was asking for. There was really only a few things one could be asking in our situation. To be free of their bounds and to run away as far away from this place as possible. I only had to wait a moment before Abigail got to work untying the rope around my wrist. Olivia might be a good killer, but she was only decent at tying rope. When the rope provided a bit of slack, I wiggled my arms up and down, managing to slip the rest of the rope off. Quickly, I reached down to my feet and unbound the rope there.

"Mmmm!"

I paid no mind to the raging redhead beside me. I had no plan to leave her here, but I needed to think of a plan if we wanted any chance of escape. Like a predator stalking their prey, I inched my way to the metal door of the shed. A quick glance outside confirmed Olivia pacing in the snow with a cellphone glued to her face. Her head furiously nodding away as I turned back to Abigail. Upon our eyes meeting, she jerked and let out a groan. If Olivia didn't kill me, Abigail certainly was going to.

I scanned the shed, trying to find anything that could help us. The single light still swinging back and forth in the shed wasn't of much help. My body tensed as I shot a look through the door to see Olivia had stopped pacing. She wasn't facing the shed anymore, but it could be any moment that she turned around and re-entered the building. If she saw that I wasn't tied up, and I didn't have a plan formed, then all that was left was being killed. But I was getting too far ahead of myself.

Trying to settle my nerves, I tried to locate something of use. The light shifted, highlighting the shovel leaning against the wall, before swinging to the other side of the shed. I moved as silently as possible to grab the shovel, pulling it up in the process. A creaking noise filled the air at my movements. I froze, eyes bulging as I waited to see what would happen next. I could no longer hear Olivia talking outside. I knew the jig was up. She would be returning any moment. I hauled the shovel up and over my shoulder, a slew of curses escaping as I did my best to hide in the corner. Hopefully, she would be too focused on Abigail that she wouldn't see me coming up from behind.

"Mmmmm!"

"What are you doing in here?" Olivia's voice called out as she shifted her body through the crack of the door and back into the shed. By instinct, I squished myself farther back in the corner, hoping that she wouldn't turn around. My hand ached from how tightly I was holding the shovel, but I'd rather deal with the pain than accidentally let the shovel go.

"I figured out what to do with you … both."

The last words coming out as a mumble as Olivia stopped. Abigail's eyes were wide as she looked at Olivia and then shifted to look at me. I swore, for Abigail had given away my position. It was as if time had slowed, adrenaline pumping through my body. Olivia swung to the side, but I was already leaping up, letting loose a battle cry as I brought the shovel down with all my might. With a loud crack, she crumpled to the ground in a heap.

"Mmmmmmm!"

I poked the downed girl with the shovel to see if she would be moving anytime soon, my grip still tight on my weapon just in case I needed to swing again. One couldn't be too careful.

"Mmmmmm!"

I tiptoed around the prone body on the ground, never taking my eyes off the girl, till I was standing right next to the redhead. I crouched, not blinking, for I didn't want to miss anything, and reached out to Abigail. Because I was more focused on the prone target than Abigail, she received a smack to the face, followed by a roaming hand while I located the cloth stuck in her mouth and tugged it out.

"Finally! Honestly, there was no need to keep this thing in my mouth!" she bellowed, but I didn't look at her. With just one look, she had given my position away. I had high confidence that if she'd had the ability to speak earlier, the ruse would have been up as soon as Olivia walked through the door. Abigail would have given the girl an earful for binding her.

"Can you untie me already?"

My grip slackened as finally I felt comfortable that Olivia would not be getting up. Not too comfortable that I didn't keep the shovel glued to my side. I still wanted that safety net just in case. With quick hands, I had Abigail free of her binds in a moment. She rubbed at her wrists before standing up with a big stretch.

"I'm never doing this again."

"Being held hostage?"

"All of this!" Abigail yelled as she waved her hands in the air. I shifted my gaze from her to the still prone figure of Olivia. If anyone wanted to be held hostage again, that would be concerning.

"We need to tie her up."

I grabbed the ropes that were once used as our own binds and made my way over to the prone figure. Winding the rope around Olivia's wrist a few times, I tied a simple knot before moving on to her feet.

"Do you even know what you are doing?"

"I'm doing my best. Never been in this kind of situation before," I bit back, trying to focus on my task at hand. I didn't need to be getting distracted and having Olivia waking up on us.

"You tied your knots all wrong. You need to include the figure eights. If you don't, she can just slide right out of them," Abigail huffed out as she bent down beside me to grab a hold of the rope that I had already wrapped around Olivia's wrist, untangling them. With skilled hands, she got them off in seconds and was working on tying the new knot. One much more elaborate than I had done the first time around.

"You know how to tie knots?"

"Of course, it comes in handy on several occasions."

My lips pursed as I looked at Abigail, who finished up tying Olivia's wrists before moving on to her ankles. I scooted back and out of her way and let her work. I wasn't sure if I really wanted to know why she had great knot tying skills, but whatever helped us ensure Olivia didn't escape and turn the tables on us would be welcomed.

"All set. I'm going back to my room. I need to book a spa treatment immediately."

"We need to carry Olivia back to the lodge."

Abigail looked down at the passed out girl before looking at me. Her face morphed into a scowl, her arms coming to cross her chest as she stared at me.

"We can't leave her here."

"Why do we need to bring her? Go get that fake cop to come get her!"

"Because we don't need her running off or we will both be back in danger."

Abigail stared at me for a moment longer before moving over to stand next to me so we could pick up Olivia. I bent towards the prone girl's head and hooked my hands under her armpits in order to pick her up. It would be a bit awkward to carry this way, but it was the only way since her hands were tied up. I shifted Olivia's weight as I waited for Abigail to pick up her feet so I wouldn't have to drag the girl through the snow back to the lodge.

"Come on!" I whined, as I looked at the redhead with me. Neither one of us would be able to go anywhere unless we brought Matt's wife with us. With a huge huff, Abigail picked up Olivia's ankles and started walking. It almost sent me tumbling to the ground from the abrupt movement. A quick pivot of my feet had us walking out the rusty shed and trekking through the snow.

"I'm tired of carrying her."

"It has only been a few minutes. We have a bit of distance to cover."

"She isn't exactly the lightest person."

I paused briefly in my steps to look at the redhead. Her cheeks were flushed, from being exposed to the cold or from overextending herself on physical activity. Regardless of the fact, she had no problem speaking what was on her mind, even it was insulting someone who was just minutes away from killing her.

"Hey!" Abigail screamed, causing me almost to drop Olivia to the ground in an attempt to cover my ears. "Hey, I'm talking to you!"

If we weren't careful and she screamed again, we might have an avalanche to deal with. I jerked forward, having to adjust my posture immediately as she let Olivia's feet drop to the ground to wave her hands in the air wildly. To the right of us was someone walking through the snow, making their way to us. He was big, and it was hard to see for the long distance between us.

"Abigail, you can't just call random people over to us," I whispered, even though the man was nowhere near to hear us.

"I'm not about to carry her all the way to the lodge when someone can help."

"Did you ever stop to think about why he is out here alone?"

She looked at me for a moment, but her expression didn't change. She was still determined to not be the one tasked with carrying the prone girl back to the lodge, even if it meant calling over a random person walking alone for help. My hold on Olivia tightened as the man's shape started to become clearer. Olivia had been on the phone with someone when I had been captured and it threw off her plans. If I got any inclination that he was somehow involved with her, we would both be in trouble. Worst-case scenario, I would run, as that was better than ending up six feet in the ground.

"What are you girls doing out here?" the man said as he finally came to a stop before us. A beanie on his head, goggles covering his eyes, and a scarf wrapped around his face, muffling his words.

"We need you to carry this girl back to the lodge."

I sighed, for Abigail didn't even explain why we had a passed-out girl with us.

"It's you!" the man chimed, bringing his hand up to lower his scarf and raise his goggles. I couldn't help but roll my eyes at the person who had come over to help us. He really did have some bad timing, almost as bad as me. For it was the same man who pointed me out when Matt was found dead. The very same man who found me in a closet with Sophia. With a bit more strength that would leave my body aching later, once all the adrenaline left, I lifted Olivia up higher as I tugged her over to the tall man.

"What happened to her?" He paused. "I knew you were trouble!"

"She isn't dead, if that is what you are asking."

"Then what did happen to her?" he asked as I dropped Olivia against him. He instantly reacted by gripping onto the shoulder of the girl as he looked at us.

"We don't have all day! I have a spa treatment waiting for me," the fiery redhead exclaimed as she took off in the direction of the lodge, successfully roping the man into helping us.

"Wait, what do you want me to do with her?"

"I already told you! Carry her!" Abigail screamed, not even stopping to look back at us as she continued on her merry way back to the lodge in order to get her spa treatment. I looked at the man beside me, who turned to look at me, but if we had free help and I didn't need to carry Olivia back, then I would gladly accept as well. With a turn, I walked after Abigail, leaving the man no choice but to pick up the prone girl and follow us back to the lodge. Sometimes it was nice having Abigail around.

# Chapter Eleven

walked up the steps of the outside patio area that would grant us entrance to the lodge. It was better than going around to the front. Abigail was a few paces ahead and had entered the lodge already. I tossed a look over my shoulder to see if the man was still following us, and he indeed was. A small chuckle escaped. I wonder what he thought of this whole situation.

He came to the mountain to enjoy his trip and instead there was a dead body. Then almost at every turn he runs into me, the main suspect of the crime.

A shouting match was the very first thing to greet me as I entered the lodge. There was a small crowd around where the shouting was coming from, but it was hard to see who exactly was yelling at each other. This mountain was just full of drama; it might be my last time coming up here. Next time, I was skipping anything dealing with mountains and staying with beaches.

"Why are you not looking for her?"

The words filling the air causing me to pause, my head tilting to the side.

"She could be dead somewhere and you are doing nothing!"

Yeah, I knew that voice. I walked towards the crowd, squeezing my way past the people who were way more focused on the drama unfolding.

"I think you meant to say she might have killed someone and they are lying dead somewhere!"

A heavy sigh escaped. I knew that voice, too. There was only one person who was adamant that I had been the one to kill Matt. I couldn't wait to see his face when we dropped the ball on him that it was Olivia. She was the true mastermind behind everything and I was just someone who got caught up in the drama for being a past lover of the man. But first, I needed to stop Sophia before she lost her mind and got herself in trouble.

"I'm okay."

"You are going to make a terrible cop!" Sophia hollered.

"Excuse me?"

"I said what I said! You aren't looking for my best friend!"

I grabbed on to Sophia's arm. She was shaking. My best friend wheeled on me. Her eyes narrowed as her lips curled into a snarl, getting ready to rip into me. Her shaking stopped, her body relaxing. With a few blinks, no doubt trying to process me showing up out of nowhere, she lunged forward, wrapping her arms around me.

"I was about to lose my mind!"

"I could tell."

I wrapped my arms around her, a chuckle escaping in the process. Sophia might be able to become an actress in the future if she really wanted to. All she needed to do was channel those real emotions and she could take off.

"Welcome back. Do you care to explain your absence?"

"I was going after the real culprit that killed Matt," I said, as I unwrapped myself from Sophia in order to stare at Jared. It was hard to believe that this man still thought I was the one at fault. I might not have liked Matt due to our breakup, but that didn't mean I would outright kill him. He was still zeroed in on me being the target that he wouldn't have come after us to help us, despite Sophia's pleas. Good thing Abigail and I took matters into our own hands, or tonight might have been a different story. Just thinking about how stubborn the man had been made me clench my jaw.

"You mean you were covering your tracks." He gave me a long stare before moving his attention to my best friend.

"If you helped her, you will be charged alongside her."

I immediately grabbed Sophia's arm, preventing her from moving from my side. We were both getting frustrated the longer we stood in Jared's presence. Her patience was already worn thin as she had been here a lot longer than I.

"Look, you aren't listening to what I am saying."

"That is because I'm reading between the lines. You are, after all, trying to throw me off."

My brain ground to a halt. It was hard to process someone with such a one track mind. I pursed my lips as I stared at Jared, who wore a satisfied smirk. Did he really think he was the smartest person in the room? If anything, it was the complete opposite, and if our conversation kept going, he would start to prove it.

"What am I supposed to do with this lady?"

I turned my attention to the man we had forced into helping us. He had finally caught up and made his way into the lodge.

"Did you kill her?" Jared shouted as he ran over to the man who had stopped walking.

"That is what I thought too, but she is definitely breathing."

Olivia was set down on one of the couches in the lodge as we all shifted to surround her. Matt's ex-wife's chest moved up and down slowly. The shovel to the head had been enough to knock her out, not kill her. I knew firsthand the damage it could inflict.

"Do you care to explain why the wife of our dead guy is passed out cold on the couch?" Jared asked as he focused his attention once more on me.

"That is what I was trying to explain."

I grabbed a chair, Jared following every movement of mine, as I brought it next to the couch of our slumbering killer in order to tell my tale. And that is what I did. I spilled everything. Almost everything. They didn't need to know exactly why Matt and I broke up and how I ended up on that mountain. That story was just a bit too embarrassing to share. But everything else was spilled into the open. I talked about reviewing the papers on each of Matt's lovers to figure out who had a motive. Jared chimed in, asking how exactly I'd obtained that evidence, a piece I'd skipped over, as that also didn't need to be told. I was trying to clear my name, not incriminate myself. The wild tale of us trying to put the pieces together, the man with the horrible timing catching us, and finally the shed incident.

"So you are saying the victim's wife killed him and tried to kill you and Abigail?"

"Yes, that is correct."

"Well, we are going to have to get the wife's side of the story. Till then you are to stay in your room."

"Wait, you don't believe me?" I hollered as I got up from my chair.

"I need all the facts before I can make a decision."

My mouth dropped, eyes bulging as I stared at the man before me. Now he wanted all the facts? Not when the dead body first appeared, but only after

I laid out hard facts in front of a roomful of people.

"Abigail was there. She can confirm everything! Wait, where is Abigail?"

I had seen her walk into the lodge before me. I was too focused on Sophia and her yelling and I had lost track of her. With a glance around, her distinct hair the color of fire was not in the lobby.

"She checked into her spa treatment."

I turned to look to see who had spoken up, and it was Charlotte making her way towards us. She cast a look down at Olivia before looking back up at me.

"So I was right? It was the wife?"

I nodded in reply. She had correctly guessed it when Jared couldn't. Just another reason he should consider a new career path and cut his losses now. It would save us all from a headache than having to deal with him later on.

"Let's get her locked up in her room. Same for you. Tomorrow we will determine the real story of what has unfolded on this mountain."

"Please carry her up to her room," Jared said to the man who had originally carried her from the shed back to the lodge. He didn't move immediately, but when he did he let out a huge sigh as he once more picked up the girl. I followed after them, Jared hot on my heels as we made our way up the stairs. It was late, and a lot had happened today. If they kept a watchful eye on Olivia tonight, then I could wait till tomorrow to set the record straight.

# Chapter Twelve

I examined myself in the bathroom mirror, for today was the day everything would be settled. I would clear my name, but most importantly, I would get Jared off my back,. It would allow me to finally start enjoying my vacation, which was actually set to end soon. So much of it had been occupied with the death of Matt and solving the case. But when life throws curveballs, they must be dealt with. With a deep breath, followed by a long exhale, I left the bathroom and made my way out of my shared bedroom with Sophia and down the stairs to the lodge.

"Good to see you didn't run off again," Jared greeted me as I entered the lobby. The day had just started, and despite being fed a bunch of facts yesterday he was still grumpy and intent on having me be the culprit. With a smile plastered on my face, I sat down next to Charlotte and Abigail, who were already present. I didn't need to wait long to prove the man wrong. Everything was about to be laid out on the table, then he would have no choice but to acknowledge that I was correct.

"Where is Olivia?"

She was the only one missing, but she was the most important person. For she was how I would clear my name. My heart rate increased, paranoid that maybe she'd escaped during the middle of the night, that Jared didn't do a good job of making sure she was locked up in her room. It wouldn't be the first time he'd failed at a job. After all, he thought I was capable of murder.

"Please open the office door and let her out," Jared called out to the employee behind the front desk, who wasted no time in turning around and opening the door. Olivia strolled out, her wrists still bound together as she joined us sitting at the table. The silence was deadly as we all stared at each other. All of us brought together once more to discuss Matt's death. This time, though, the outcome would be different. I glanced in the direction of Abigail, who was seated to my right. She looked to be extremely pissed off, arms across her chest as she leaned back in her seat, her face set in a scowl as she looked at Olivia. I couldn't blame her for being pissed off. Being tied up, dragged through the snow, and then put in a rusty shed to die would piss off the nicest of people.

Charlotte was the least bothered out of all the people at the table. She also had the least amount of involvement in the death of the cheating man. Her face was neutral; it was just another day for her. Maybe not exactly normal. It wasn't like people just dropped dead often.

"So, girls, who would like to start?" asked Jared.

"Why am I even here? We all know you did it," Abigail bit out as she set Olivia with a glare. "I almost missed my spa treatment because of you."

"Olivia, would you like to defend yourself?"

She looked to Jared, before looking at each of us at the table, her eyes narrowing as they landed on me.

"You weren't supposed to show up. That wasn't part of the plan."

"Going to jail for a crime I didn't commit wasn't part of my vacation plan," I replied. Did she really think I would just accept the guilty verdict and go to jail? A chuckle escaped, but was quickly silenced when Jared spoke up.

"Olivia, are you saying that you had a hand in Matt's death?"

"No."

"Then did Brittany have a hand in Matt's death?"

"Wait, you still think I did it?" I exclaimed as I jumped out of my seat, my hands slamming down on the table as I glared at Jared.

"I will be asking the questions. Take your seat."

I fell back into my seat in a huff. I was sure that by capturing Olivia it would be clear to all those involved that it was her. She had tried to kill Abigail and me! Why couldn't he see it?

"Olivia, I will ask again. Did you have anything to do with Matt's death?"

She shook her head no. This time, instead of the outrage coming from me, it came from Abigail.

"Just go ahead and lock her up! I have things I need to do," Abigail said, her voice coming out in a whine. Jared looked at her for a moment before setting his gaze once more on Olivia.

"Olivia, if you are found guilty, you will be charged with murder, attempted murder, and kidnapping."

This time, with the re-enforcement from Abigail, Jared was finally listening and understanding. I wasn't the culprit. It shouldn't have needed to come to this, but I would take whatever help at this point.

"Wait, you can't send me to jail!" Olivia shouted as she shifted in her seat, almost falling out in her haste to look at Jared. "I didn't do what you said I did!" Being faced with going to jail could make anyone crumble. Olivia threw out her hands to latch on to Jared's arm as she tugged herself up from her seat.

"I swear! I didn't kill anyone! I wasn't even going to kill them!"

"What do you call hitting me on the head with a shovel and tying us up in the shed?"

"I just needed to delay for a bit of time!"

"Walk us through your plan," Charlotte piped up next to me. She was leaning in, her chest brushed against the rim of the table. Out of everyone involved, she was the one who correctly guessed Olivia was the culprit. Now all we needed to do was figure out why.

With a heavy sigh, the main target of our attention fell back in her seat. She attempted to push back her hair, but her wrist tied up made it awkward.

"It was a simple plan, really. Get Abigail to invest in Matt's business so we could collect the money…" After a breath of pause, she continued: "…fake Matt's death in order to collect the life insurance, and make sure Abigail saw his death so she would think her money was lost." She turned to me before speaking once again. "You were an easy target to blame. We didn't think you would actually do anything to look into the crime."

"What made you think I would just accept going to jail?" I countered, annoyed that they'd pegged me as such a pushover.

"Um, excuse me, what do you mean by fake Matt's death?" Charlotte interrupted. I looked to my left at the blond girl. I had missed that part. A bit too focused on the fact they thought I was easy prey.

"Matt isn't dead. That is why you can't send me to jail for murder!"

"If Matt is not dead ... where is he?"

"Obviously Matt is dead! He is in the freezer!" Jared said, his pace erratic as he turned away from the table. We wasted no time in following after the soon-to-be cop to see where he was going. If Matt was truly not dead, then the whole story changed. He was in on it. That was obvious. But where had he been for the past few days?

Jared headed to the restaurant area, pushing past the front counter. The employees went to speak up, but with a raised hand from Charlotte they went back to work. It was a good thing we had the boss on our side. Past the counter and the employees cooking, Jared stopped before a walk-in freezer. My face scrunched up. Is that where they had kept the body the whole time? Nausea formed as Jared opened the door. I could only hope that our food was not stored in the same freezer as the dead guy or I would throw up. Well, the supposedly dead guy.

We stood to the side with bated breath as Jared entered. A minute later he re-emerged, his face set, not giving away any indication of what might or might not be in the freezer. I waited to see if he would spill the beans or if Olivia had truly killed Matt, but he didn't talk, opting to just pace back and forth. Dread replaced the nausea as I walked into the freezer. On one hand, I was relieved that there wasn't food in the freezer. But on the other hand, there also was no body.

"There is no body," I called as I left the freezer, closing the door behind me.

"See! You can't charge me for murder if he isn't dead!"

"Jared, you did check to confirm he was dead, right?" I pressed.

"Everyone said he was dead."

"But we aren't the ones studying to be a cop ... so shouldn't you confirm he was actually dead?"

"He wasn't moving."

"Just because someone isn't moving doesn't mean they are dead..." I said slowly, my tone condescending. It was hard to process the turn of events. This whole time Jared pinned me as the culprit for the murder of Matt, for a guy who wasn't even dead! If he had focused a bit more on solving the crime, he would have noticed there was no dead body, but now we had a new mystery to solve.

Where was Matt Jones?

# Chapter Thirteen

The lodge was packed, everyone standing shoulder to shoulder as an emergency meeting had been called. The employees of the lodge had made an announcement and went door to door to gather all the visitors together.

"You think Jared will make a fool of himself?"

"No way. He probably will make himself look like a hero," I replied to Sophia, who stood squished to my side. As if he could hear himself being talked about, Jared had emerged from the office behind the counter. With the help of a chair, he stepped onto the front desk so he could have a view over the whole crowd. He scanned the area, and I wondered if he really thought Matt would join us. The man had managed to dupe everyone and have people think he was dead. He wouldn't get caught so easily by standing in a lobby full of people.

"We have an announcement to make. Please stay calm," Jared started, which had the opposite effect, for people started to murmur. A snort escaped me, as this was getting off to a bad start, but what else could be expected when the wannabe cop was involved.

"We have solved the case of the murder of Matt Jones, the man found on the deck a few days ago." Jared paused, his hands raising as he patted the air to get the crowd to calm down.

"It turns out Matt Jones is actually not dead and there was no murder committed."

There was an uproar now, as people voiced their confusion. Jared was taking his sweet time and going about things in a roundabout way. If I wasn't directly involved in what had unfolded, I would be just as confused.

"But there have been quite a few crimes committed at this resort. Financial fraud and kidnapping with attempted murder and insurance fraud under investigation."

I wanted to smack my face. While there might not have been a murder, there was a kidnapping with attempted murder. Those things were almost equal, so while someone might have not died, someone came very close. Namely Abigail and I.

"What is going on?"

Someone voiced the opinion of the crowd as everyone else nodded their head in agreement.

"It seems there is more than meets the eye on this case up on this mountain."

"Are we safe?"

"Well, technically, we don't know where Matt Jones, our supposed to be dead guy, is at this moment," Jared started, but soon realized his mistake as everyone started to shout. "Don't worry though, we will find him! We just need all of your help to do so."

Not only would Jared make a horrible cop, he would also be terrible at giving speeches. Nothing about what he said was comforting. Then asking the people to help track down someone on a mountain where the real cops were nowhere to be found due to the weather was a tall ask.

"We will separate into groups in order to search the lodge and surrounding areas."

With no other instructions, Jared jumped off the front desk to the floor. Employees emerged and started sorting us into groups. Each group was assigned areas. Some to the slopes, the lodge, and the area outside the lodge.

"Can't believe there is more to the story. Goodbye vacation time."

"Yeah, makes me wonder if I should just avoid vacations," I replied to my best friend as we got sorted into the group that would search the building.

"I see we are in the same group."

I turned to see who had spoken up, only to lay eyes on the man with the bad timing. He had carried Olivia back to her lodge yesterday and now he was in our group to hunt down Matt.

"I was starting to have my doubts about you being a killer."

"And I was starting to have my doubts about you being a stalker," I replied. It was true, he was a bit of a stalker, always arriving at the perfect time. But just like me, who just happened to be on this mountain and used as easy prey, he was just someone who appeared at the wrong time. Multiple times.

"Glad you had a change of heart, though. Now we need to find the true mastermind behind all of this."

The man nodded as he walked ahead of the group. Time passed at a snail's pace as we searched every inch of the lodge. There was no corner left unchecked. Everything was moved just in case there was a hiding spot we weren't aware of. But every group turned up empty. There wasn't one hint that Matt was still on the mountain with us. He had somehow managed to make it back to civilization while the police had a hard time even making it up here. I would give it to the man, he was dedicated. I threw myself back on one of the couches in the lodge as Jared went around collecting any tidbits of information people could provide. Which, by the frustrated sighs and exclamation at having to spend their vacation time searching for someone who wasn't even on the mountain, was a lot of nothing.

"I think all this hard work deserves some apple cider, don't you think?"

"Of course all you can think about is the apple cider!"

"I'm trying to get my fill before we go back to Florida. They don't do apple cider the same as the north."

My short rest on the couch morphed into us getting up to go stand in line for two cups of hot apple cider. I had to agree with Sophia, though. The apple cider down south didn't compare with what they provided up here. Maybe it was the weather that added to the coziness of the drink, but whatever it was had us coming back several times throughout our trip for a cup of the hot, delicious liquid.

With our prize in hand, we both headed outside to the deck, where the bonfire was located. We weren't the only ones trying to enjoy the last of our day, since most of it was spent searching. An empty bonfire drew our attention as we made our way over there. I was glad to finally be able to sit back and enjoy some relaxation. Tomorrow the day would repeat and we would have to work on the mystery once more. But today was a win. I had finally cleared my name and I was no longer the prime suspect with the fake death of Matt Jones. A small chuckle escaped as I brought the apple cider to my lips for a drink. Everything that had happened was a weird, twisted turn of events, but it had been fun. Even if my life was on the line.

# Chapter Fourteen

There wasn't a town hall meeting today in the lodge. But that wasn't from the lack of trying. From some of the employees mumbling about, Jared had attempted to call upon the guests of the lodge once more, but this time people refused the call. I couldn't blame them, they wanted to enjoy their vacation—something of mine that was being cut very short. I sat at one of the empty tables with Sophia as we waited for everything to be sorted out. The weather had finally cleared, allowing transport to happen down the mountain. Which meant we could all go down to repeat the story for the police, who were, hopefully, much more capable people than Jared. He did have a change of heart and was easier to work with once all the facts were laid out in front of him. But it took some annoying words from the redhead who was fed up with the whole situation to get it drilled into his skull that it wasn't me who he should be worried about.

"Our vacation was no vacation at all."

"At least Charlotte offered to cover the bill so we wouldn't have to pay anything."

"So, should we come back again?" Sophia replied as she looked over at me. I turned to look at her, watching her expression for a moment, before we both burst out laughing. There was no way we were returning to this mountain. We had learned our lesson. We would not be repeating our mistakes. We would have to find another remote mountain that no one had ever heard about and hope that others didn't show up as well.

I let loose a deep sigh as I shoved my hands into the pockets of my jacket. Soon I would be able to shed my winter gear and put back on clothes suitable for the beach, but that would be a few days away. First, we had to get through the police questioning, then I would be free.

"Ready, girls?" Jared piped up as he turned from the front counter after settling his bill. Charlotte had only covered half his bill; he had to pay the rest. Sophia and I stood, grabbing our luggage as we followed him out the front doors and to the shuttle that would take us down. Olivia, along with Abigail, was already situated in the shuttle with several suitcases. Our redheaded friend had needed to receive assistance to load all her bags, for she didn't want to do it herself. According to her, it would have made all the spa appointments she paid for pointless.

"Finally, we're leaving. I was about to tell the driver to leave you all behind," Abigail said as she leaned back in her seat, crossing her legs. I paid her no attention. We had a long journey ahead of us, for it took a few hours to make it down the mountain. There would be no point in poking the bear when trapped in an enclosed space with it.

Time passed slowly as we made our way down the winding trail that had a few scary parts—but the driver was experienced. As we got closer to the end of the road, where a city could be found, I couldn't help but wonder how exactly did Matt make it off the mountain. There wasn't any transportation working till today, so that option was out. Unless someone made the drive up to get him, which was also unlikely, as the police would have had a word with whoever was about to make such a dangerous drive up. My nose crinkled as the only feasible but also super outrageous answer was that he'd trekked down the mountain. Was Matt that crazy to do that? What was I saying—of course he was. He had tricked Abigail into investing in his make-believe business, got his wife to go along with his outrageous plan of pretending that he died so they could collect on life insurance, then used me as a scapegoat after giving me the most humiliating breakup of my life. I huffed, folding my arms across my chest. Matt was definitely crazy enough to walk down the mountain. I was lucky to have dodged that bullet.

The shuttle jerked to a stop as we finally made it to the city. It was a cozy little city that didn't get much traffic unless people passed by in order to get to the resort.

"I will be checking in on Olivia, then the three of you will need to show up for questioning," Jared said as he reached for Olivia and helped her out of her seat. After the announcement that it was impossible to find Matt on the mountain, she had broken down in tears. Her husband was treating her like a scapegoat, like how they attempted to treat me. I felt a little bad for her—only a little though. Karma had made a full circle and slammed right into her face.

I grabbed my bag and quickly exited the shuttle as Abigail roped the shuttle driver into helping her unload her suitcases. Our vacation that wasn't too much of a vacation had been cut short, all due to a past lover. Once we finished at the police station, we had the option of going back up to the mountain. Charlotte had graciously said she would pay for a few extra nights since we didn't get to enjoy ours. But Sophia and I were in an agreement, we'd had enough of an adventure for now.

I took in the town. There wasn't much to it. There were a few shops by the shuttle stop. Namely, a bar and a small convenience store. Maybe I should buy a souvenir to take home to remember this whole adventure. A laugh escaped. Who was I kidding, I was never going to forget this.

"All set?" Sophia chimed as she was finally able to escape the shuttle after Abigail had all her bags unloaded. I nodded to Sophia, reaching out to grab my luggage. With one last glance around, taking in the town, I went to follow my best friend to the police station. There I paused. There was a tickle in the back of my head, begging for me to turn back around.

I looked back at the convenience store, but nothing grabbed my attention. When I turned to the outside bar, though, I froze in my tracks, for I'd remember that mop of hair anywhere. The man shifted as he picked up his cup to take a drink, and I knew right then and there it was Matt Jones. That sneaky man had indeed made it off the mountain, with none of us noticing till the last minute.

"Sophia," I hissed, beckoning my friend to my side. She paused for a moment before coming to stand beside me. I pointed in the direction of the bar to the man still situated at the counter.

"Is that ... who I think it is?" Her words were low as she spoke. We didn't want to tip him off that he had been found. That his carefully crafted plan had fallen to pieces in the last moments.

"It is!"

"What do we do? We need to get the cops!"

I looked at Matt and then in the direction of the police station. We needed a distraction to keep him busy and at the bar long enough for the police to come. I looked at my best friend, her mouth curving into a smile. I knew she was thinking what I was thinking. We would need another dramatic display, but this time I patted my friend's shoulder, for she would not be the star. Instead, I shifted my attention to the girl with the red hair who was still very pissed off about her money and the fact that she had been kidnapped. A laugh escaped as I walked over to Abigail, who looked up from trying to get reception on her phone.

"What do you want?"

"Isn't that Matt over there?" I called with a sweet voice, doing my best to act as innocent as possible. Her head whipped around, trying to locate the man, and I pointed in the direction of the bar. She locked on to the back of Matt's head, and when he took another chug from his drink, it provided the perfect side profile of his face. Without missing a beat and without a care in the world that her luggage was on the side of the road, she stormed off in the direction of the bar.

With a satisfied smile on my face, I bounced back over to Sophia, grabbing a hold of my luggage.

"Do you think that was wise?"

"She deserves some alone time with him after everything she went through, don't you think?"

Sophia followed after me as we headed in the direction of the police station. The once quiet city on the side of the mountain was soon filled with screaming, as I knew Abigail had gotten her hands on Matt. He had poked the bear and there was no escape—until I sent the cops over—but I would take my sweet time walking to the station. After all, he had left me to fend for myself for days. He could survive for a few minutes.

—*ele*—

Thank you for reading Stiff Competition! You can find additional books by me here: https://www.irisleigh.com/book-list/

# About Iris Leigh

Iris Leigh stumbled upon the genre of cozy mystery by accident. Since Iris is easily scared she does her best to avoid horror books, tv shows, and films. But dying for some type of mystery without all the suspense to make her heart burst from terror was when someone asked if she had ever read a cozy mystery. Now she has fallen in love with the genre and started to write to bring her stories to life.

If you want to stay in contact with Iris and learn about upcoming releases, make sure to sign up for her newsletter! You can sign up by navigating to her website!

Website: www.irisleigh.com

# Also By Iris Leigh

A Cat Aunt Cozy Mystery

Tabby Trouble

Himalayan Heist

Persian Pursuit

# Newsletter Sign Up!

235